MADNESS BY FIRELIGHT
13 TALES TO KEEP YOU UP AT NIGHT

Edited by **MICHAEL BERTOLINI**

All content is fictitious; names and places are either fictitious or used in a fictitious manner. All rights reserved. Content may not be reused or stored in any system retrieval device, known or unknown, without prior permission from the copyright holder. This book, nor any part of it, may be resold in any format without prior consent of the publisher. If you have any questions or concerns, or would like to reach any of the authors here-in, please contact M Presents at the address below.

M Presents
542 Hopmeadow St 116
Simsbury, CT 06070
mpresentpublishing.com

Copyright 2024

Up All Night…	1
Deep Cover…	13
The Resurrectionist…	61
Growing Pains…	93
The Brides…	117
In The Shadows…	133
The Wraithwood Weaver…	146
Island Of The Moggie…	161
The Cairn…	178
It Really Isn't Safe Out There…	196
Vixen…	210
The Wrong Turn…	233
Thirty Minutes…	257

EDITOR'S INTRODUCTION

You're sitting around the campfire; it's dark, the moon is high in the sky, the wind is whistling through the trees, and the sense of isolation is pervasive. You hear a twig snap in the darkness, everyone is tense. What's the story you tell your friends to terrify them? What's in the dark, stalking the camp: an ax murderer, a werewolf, or something so far beyond our mortal understanding that just the sight of it will drive each of us insane?

That's the general prompt I asked for when I announced the submission call for this book. Since the dawn of civilization, people have gathered around campfires to share stories—some to scare children and others to preserve tales handed down through generations. These flickering flames have cast shadows on the faces of storytellers and their rapt audiences, creating an atmosphere where the boundaries between reality and imagination blur. The stories told around these campfires have become an essential part of human culture, a way to connect with the past, entertain the present, and shape the future. They are not just stories; they are the echoes of our ancestors, the whispers of history, and the fears that bind us all.

While not all stories are told around a campfire, and this book doesn't feature an overarching narrative in that sense, storytelling remains a timeless tradition we cherish. It transcends the medium, whether it be the warmth of a campfire, the glow of a flashlight under the covers, or the quiet rustle of pages in a dimly lit room. Storytelling is an act of sharing, of creating connections, and of exploring the unknown. How many of us have heard a tale that a narrator claimed to have heard from a friend's brother's cousin, about something that happened in these very woods on a night just like tonight? These tales, often exaggerated and embellished with each retelling, become legends in their own right, adding to the rich tapestry of human folklore.

Previous stories in this series have had specific focuses, from the biting cold of winter to a creeping sense of madness. Each tale was crafted to evoke a particular emotion, to transport the reader to a different world, and to leave a lasting impression. But this time, I wanted to be very clear about my expectations: I wanted to be scared, not just unsettled or discomforted. I craved stories that would make my heart race, my palms sweat, and my breath catch in my throat. I longed for the thrill of the unknown, the fear of the unseen, and the terror of the inexplicable. I wanted to delve into the darkest corners of the human psyche, to confront the fears that lurk in the shadows, and to experience the full spectrum of horror.

I wanted ghosts, goblins, and unfathomable eldritch horrors from the depths of space and time. I yearned for tales that would transport me to haunted houses, cursed forests, and otherworldly realms where the laws of nature no longer apply. I wanted to feel the fear, to experience the characters' terror, and to sense that overwhelming dread that comes from facing the unknown. I wanted stories that would stay with me long after I had finished reading, that would haunt my dreams and make me question what is real and what is imagined.

These stories, which have reached into the darkest corners of my heart and torn down the walls to let shadows spread, will drive you to the brink of madness! They are not for the faint of heart, but for those who seek the thrill of fear, the excitement of the unknown, and the challenge of confronting their deepest fears. They are a testament to the power of storytelling, to the ability of words to evoke emotions, and to the timeless appeal of horror.

Or, at the very least, they'll give you a reason to share them with everyone you know and encourage them to pick up their own copy of this book. What is a story if not shared? What is fear if not experienced together? These tales are meant to be discussed, dissected, and debated. They are meant to be passed on, to inspire new stories, and to keep the tradition of storytelling alive.

Promotional intentions aside, my true desire was to create a horror book. M Presents emerged from my passion for the genre, and I can't get enough of it. Horror has always fascinated me, not just for its ability to scare, but for its ability to explore the human condition. It delves into our deepest fears, our darkest desires, and our most primal instincts. It forces us to confront the unknown, to question our reality, and to explore the boundaries of our imagination.

So, as you delve into these stories, I hope you enjoy them as much as I have. Sleep with the light on, close your closet door, and ignore those whispers from under your bed. Allow yourself to be transported to different worlds, to experience different fears, and to confront different horrors. Let these tales take you on a journey into the unknown, and allow yourself to be scared, thrilled, and mesmerized.

Remember, these stories are not just about fear; they are about the thrill of the unknown, the excitement of the unexpected, and the joy of a well-told tale. They are about the power of storytelling, the magic of words, and the timeless appeal of horror. So sit back, relax, and enjoy the ride. But be warned: once you start, you may not be able to stop.

And who knows? You may find yourself telling these stories around a campfire one day, passing them on to the next generation, and keeping the tradition of storytelling alive. Because in the end, that is what these stories are all about: connecting with the past, entertaining the present, and shaping the future. They are about the power of fear, the magic of words, and the timeless appeal of a well-told tale. So enjoy these stories, share them with others, and keep the tradition of storytelling alive.

-Michael Bertolini
2024

UP ALL NIGHT
Riley Santangelo

We found the campsite during a muggy Florida May, the yellow flies buzzing and biting and completely ignoring the organic bug spray we'd doused ourselves in. The wooden shelter was two stories tall with a screened-in room at the bottom, a ladder, and a trap door leading up to a loft on top.

I climbed up and peeked into the loft. It was a small, attic-like space with a handful of mats on the ground, and mesh-covered windows spilling muted sunlight and illuminating dancing dust motes. It wasn't fancy, but there were no spider webs in the corners, and it had a hook-and-eye latch on the door. It could make for a cozy overnight space.

We decided we would stay there later in the year, maybe in October or November when it was cooler out. In the meantime, we came back to the trail once every few weeks and visited the swamp, taking pictures of the alligator hatchlings and pygmy rattlers we'd pass along the way. Each time saw us more prepared than the last. The hiking trail was about a mile off of the main road and cars weren't permitted into the park, the road barred by a solid metal barrier. So we started bringing bikes and packs full of water bottles and bug spray. We started dressing in long sleeves and hats and pants that we'd tuck into snake-proof boots.

    We had a plan. We would wait until a dry weekend, each bringing a large pack with a blanket and pillow, water, bug spray, and snacks. Flashlights and a first aid kit, if needed. There was no cell service out in the park, so it would be a perfect opportunity to unplug from everyone and everything. We both needed it.

    Hurricane season came and went, and mid-November brought cooler air and chill nights. We shared our plan with a few select people, like Cee's aunt and my mom. *Rice Creek Preserve,* I texted her. *Staying overnight, no cell service. Love you!*

At 3:15 on a Saturday, we packed our gear and headed out. The parking lot was completely deserted when we pulled up, which wasn't unusual. We'd only ever passed one other couple during our visits. It eased my anxiety about having to fight over the shelter with someone else. It was first come, first serve, and there was no guarantee that the campsite would be available when we wanted it. But sure enough, the road into the preserve was empty, the trail deserted save for the sparkling webs of banana spiders. We ducked under and around them, careful not to disturb them.

At the campsite, Cee locked our bikes to a trail marker sign and I found the trail log stashed in a wooden box by the picnic table. I flipped to the most recent entry left two weeks ago. *Heard a Barred Owl in the night*, they wrote. *Left a James Patterson in the shelter, pass it along! Over and out, Geezer.*

"Should we give ourselves trail names?" I asked.

Cee considered. "I think you have to earn those or something."

"Like biker gang nicknames?"

"Yeah," she said. "Like you have to break your ankle on the trail first, and then you can be called Lefty."

I snorted. "Cool. Let's aim for something less dramatic. Like maybe Blisters and Sunburn."

For now, I signed my entry with *L & C* and left it at that.

We left our packs in the loft to wander the trail, confident that no one would come by and take anything. The weather was too brisk for alligators or snakes, and the crunch of leaves under our boots meant we scared off almost any other wildlife save for the occasional bird. Before long, our wandering led us back to the campsite, where we decided to start a fire and eat before it got too dark.

Cee conjured fire from nearly nothing and we sat side by side at its edge. I leaned my head on her shoulder and we listened to the sounds of the night gathering around us. It was peaceful. I spotted the first lightning bug off in the trees, thinking my eyes were playing tricks on me.

"Look," I said, and then suddenly they were all around us, dancing and blinking like Christmas come early.

Full dark came around 6:30, the waning moon illuminating little through the thick trees. Neither of us was tired, but we both felt we'd be safer up in the loft where we could observe nature through a set of walls, eight feet off the ground.

We used our phone flashlights to set up our makeshift beds. The meager latch closed the trapdoor from the inside, which made me feel a bit more secure, though Cee said it wouldn't keep anyone out. "Should have brought a drill and screwed it shut for the night," she said. I knew she wasn't joking.

She rolled onto her side with her head on my pillow and we lay silently, listening to the droning of crickets and frogs and late cicadas.

"I'm glad we did this," Cee whispered.

"Me too."

We lay listening for a time. Here, an owl. There, a crackling of the fire, a snapping limb under the feet of some creature or other. We fell asleep lulled by the unsteady susurrus of the wind through the trees and the many-mouthed murmur of the forest.

Hours later, I was awoken by a sound and sat bolt upright. Cee grabbed my wrist. I could just barely make out her outline in the dark.

"What—" I started, but she squeezed, silencing me.

Another sound, ill-defined and animal. It was beneath us.

My heart raced and my head spun. I tried to shake off sleep and gain context from my meager bearings. *What is that,* I wanted to shout. I tried to steady my breathing as the two of us sat stock-still, listening.

A wuffling sort of noise from below. Creaking wood. A crunch of leaves. Heavy. Instinctively, I reached for my phone. It was zipped into my pack, though. No service anyway.

"What is it," I whispered, as softly as I could. *"A bear?"*

Cee was breathing heavily through her nose. "Could be. Maybe a black bear. The food is all up here with us."

"Shit," I breathed.

There was a vibration through the floor, a soft swaying. "The ladder," she said.

I didn't think. I lunged for my pack and pushed it on top of the trapdoor.

"Lea," she hissed. I went for her pack as well and started gathering our heavy boots and water bottles, the extra

sleeping pads. Our blankets and pillows, light as they were. All of them over the door and its tiny latch. On hands and knees, we both scrambled to the other side of the loft and flattened ourselves against the opposite wall. *Thump,* went the door. The mound of gear atop it wobbled. *Thump. Thump.*

I started crying, soundlessly. "What is that? What do we do?"

"I don't know," Cee said, quavering. She was crying too. I grabbed her hand.

The scratching began on the underside of the door. Slow, at first, one long scrape from back to front. Again. And again. Cee sobbed, once. I squeezed her hand. Felt the frenzied throb of her pulse beneath my thumb.

The scratching got faster, and erratic. Two sets of claws now, each harder than the last, our packs thumping up and down, shifting and sliding. I could feel the panic closing in, choking me, sucking the air from my lungs. Maybe I'd pass out. Maybe I'd drown.

Cee had her arm out, that protective stance against an unknown threat. *"Cee,"* I hissed, but she wasn't going anywhere. She just wanted to put herself between me and danger. I leaned in and wrapped both arms around her, pulling her close to me. I was more frightened of her leaving my side.

A sudden silence filled the space, our heavy breaths the only sound above the roaring in my ears. Cee craned her neck to look out the screened window and I turned, straining my eyes to make out shapes in the dark. The soft light of the moon gave outlines to trees beyond our circle of campsite, but nothing moved.

Do you think it's gone, I wanted to ask, but the noises had stopped so suddenly. Surely we'd have heard the snap of twigs, and the crunch of leaves beneath its retreating feet, if it were truly gone.

And suddenly the barrage started again. Thumping, rhythmic, and unsteady. Dragging scrapes along the underside of the floor, starting from one end of the loft to the other, getting ever closer to us at the far end before retreating again. *"What is it,"* Cee cried. *"What the fuck is it?"* I clutched her body closer.

The latch held as the little hook clinked against its eye. *Thwap, thwap, thwap. Scratch. Thwap, thwap, thwap, scratch*. We cried and shook, and I held her tight. We didn't sleep. It didn't stop.

Hours passed in delirium. We tried both of our phones, but neither any help. We strategized about climbing out the tiny window, furious whispers in the dark eventually leading to the conclusion that no, we were safer up here. The meager latch wouldn't hold forever, though, and Cee ended up lying atop the door. I pulled a mat over and lay over it next to her. Our bodies jumped and shook with the rattling beneath us. I felt I should have run out of tears by now, that surely I would have run out of the 70% water my body had to offer.

We exchanged hushed *I love yous. I'm sorrys. If onlys.* If only I hadn't taken this job that left me stressed and anxious, in need of an out. If only we'd thought to read up on surviving bear encounters. If only Cee had brought that goddamned drill along to screw the door tightly shut.

But dawn finally began to break, the first luminous tendrils of it turning Cee's hair golden at the edges, and the thing, whatever it was, eventually stopped.

We felt the shaking of the ladder beneath our weary bodies and remained there, hushed, tense, not daring to trust the fading sound of crackling pine needles as it retreated into the trees. We lay there, silent and still and huffing exhausted breaths for hours more until the sun itself was just visible through the window.

"Do you think it's gone?" I dared to whisper, and Cee said she didn't know.

We turned and peeked our eyes out just above the windowsill. The ground was dewey and everything shimmered in the early morning sunlight. Birds were chirping. A Mourning Dove cooed, just outside. But nothing else stirred, no movement or sound came below us or at the tree line.

"We pack everything up. Tight. Make sure you've got a good grip on it," Cee said. "Get your boots on. Leave everything you can't carry on your back. I'm just going to look out. But be ready to slam the door down."

I swallowed and nodded. She crouched over the trapdoor and paused. Then lifted it, ever so slowly. No movement. No shapes. The coast looked clear.

Cee would go down first. I would toss the packs down and we'd unlock the bikes as quickly as we could, pedal the mile back to our car like our lives depended on it.

"Ready?" she asked, but she was up and climbing down the hatch before I had a chance to respond. "It's fine!" she called up from below. "Come on."

I shoved our packs down through the opening and descended, boots slipping in the dust. Grabbed my pack and hoisted it onto my back without noticing its weight. "Come on," I echoed, running to the bikes. What the hell was the combination again, and why had we thought it was so important to lock them up? I finally remembered, and the lock slid apart. I tossed the chain on the ground, meaning to just leave it for now. "I got it," I said, turning to hold Cee's bike out for her to take, but she wasn't there.

"Cee?" I saw her, back to me, standing at the picnic table. "Hey, come on!" I called and hurried over to her.

She was looking down at the trail log. It lay open there on the table, though I was certain I'd put it back in its box last night.

"Cee?" I said again, coming to look over her shoulder.

It was open to the last page, to my entry from yesterday. Under my words in the log, in an unfamiliar scrawl, one line had been written:

Hope I didn't keep you up all night.

DEEP COVER
Brit Jones

The banker was on his knees in the forest clearing, wrists, ankles, and mouth secured by duct tape. He was whimpering. Six men were standing around him. They were in fatigues and had carbines slung over their shoulders as well as side arms. One had his pistol in his hand.

"Well, go ahead and do it, man," said Moss.

"Screw you. If you're so hot and bothered to see it done, you do it," said Green.

Green looked around at the others. They were fidgeting uncomfortably, not meeting his eyes. Except Jenkins. Jenkins met his gaze dispassionately. Jenkins wasn't fidgeting at all. Jenkins gave them all the creeps. He had told them he was a veteran of multiple tours in Iraq and Afghanistan. He wouldn't elaborate on what he had done there, but the others had thought it was something hot. Jenkins was unflappable and seemingly devoid of emotion.

They'd taken him on based on his military training and the fact that he talked a convincing line about hating Jews, blacks, Arabs, and Hispanics. More than one of them had come to regret the decision. But none of the others had any sort of military background and considered him a good resource for training purposes. Out in the Oregon forest, he had given them rudimentary training on the use of carbines and pistols. They were far from proficient.

The tape over the banker's mouth came loose.

"…may my death serve as an atonement for all sins that I have committed before You. May You grant me a position in Paradise and enable me to merit life in the world to come which is set aside for the righteous. Hear O Israel, the Lord is our God, the Lord is One…"

Moss and Green were still arguing about who was going to kill the Jewish banker. Jenkins walked over and said, "Give me the pistol."

Green handed it over. Jenkins walked behind the banker and shot him in the back of the head. The others stood around with their mouths half open. None of them had seen a man killed before.

"The rest of you dismember the body. Hands, feet, and head. Stuff shotgun shells into his mouth and fire a shot into it. No dental records. Not much of a head either. Bury the parts several miles apart from one another and do it deep so animals don't get at it."

"Who put you in charge?" Graham growled. He was a large, burly man whom the others deferred to as the natural alpha. Jenkins did not.

"Graham, when you or one of these others put a bullet through a man's skull I'll take up clean-up duty. For now, it falls on you five."

Graham glared at Jenkins. Jenkins met his eyes without expression. Graham looked away.

"Alright, guys. Get out the saws and let's get to work."

Jenkins was going to have to come up with a story to explain this whole fiasco to his handler in Portland. He was just supposed to be an informant, not a participant. But a week in the wilderness with this group of idiots had rubbed his last nerve raw.

He was half-Jewish. He had served with blacks and Hispanics in the service. He had made friendly connections with Arab interpreters. He didn't hate anybody based on their race. He did hate incompetents like the ones he had been saddled with.

***

He missed the desert. Things were simple there. There were the bad guys and the good guys and you generally knew which was which. There was collateral damage, but it was war. These things happened. He had advanced and been made Long Range Reconnaissance Patrol. He spent weeks in the desert by himself, scouting, making contact with tribal elders, and establishing enemy movements. Purely in his element, he thrived. A firefight with five Taliban, in which he didn't get a scratch and ended with the five enemy dead, and four wounded GIs rescued, earned him a Bronze Star.

After that, he started staying out longer than he was supposed to. He killed more Taliban, more insurgents, and didn't report it. The desert was clean and became his home.

He got dressed down when he would post late but didn't care. He was cited for insubordination but didn't care. Being on base made him nervous and antsy. Ha craved the solitude of the desert.

One night after a long patrol they came to him. They whispered in his ear. They told him that a village a mile away was a Taliban holdout. They told him he had to act. He did. He killed every man and boy child in that village, sparing only the women and girl children. Women and children had died by his hand previously. He had become a hard man, but not so hard that he would keep voluntarily killing little girls. There was still collateral. It was war. These things happened.

They came to him again. They were displeased that he had let the females live. He told them to fuck off and called for emergency evac. When the chopper landed they found him covered in blood surrounded by a pile of corpses and a crowd of wailing women.

They airlifted him to Germany, where he underwent a psychological profile and was deemed unfit for further duty. As a decorated Marine he was given a discharge with full honors and the situation in the village was buried.

The Department of Justice contacted him straight off the transport to recruit him. They used terms like "domestic terrorism" and the "white nationalist threat". They said that the country was in more danger from an attack originating domestically than from anywhere in the Middle East. He was to infiltrate these groups and report on sedition or plans for terror attacks, kidnappings, or assassinations. Since he had no idea what he was going to do back in the world, he agreed.

They flew him to Portland, where he met his handler. Jeanine was her name. She was cold as ice. He was assigned to infiltrate a nascent group of white nationalists and monitor their progress. He pressed for something more challenging, but she told him as the newest, despite his experience, he would have to earn his stripes before being given something more challenging. So he was assigned to the group of incompetents he had now. He was convinced if the banker hadn't been drunk coming out of the whorehouse at four in the morning they would have blown the operation. It was still he who put the man in a chokehold and got him into the van before he could make any noise.

***

They seemed to do a relatively good job at disposing of the corpse, but that didn't give him any more faith in them. He was on watch duty at 3 am, which he found preposterous considering that no one knew where they were. Leaning against a tree with a carbine on his lap, half dozing, he was suddenly wide awake. A familiar slithering, slavering sound came from the underbrush near the tree. The thing stayed in the shadows, out of the dim light of the guttering campfire.

"Jenkins", it hissed. "We are missing you."

"I thought I left you in the desert. How the fuck did you find me?"

"Finding if we're wanting to."

"What do you want from me, anyway?"

"Join us. Long, long life. Do things you're best at."

"And what would that be?"

The thing laughed, a gurgling, wet sound.

"Taking lives, Jenkins. You took many in the desert. Then take the souls. The most delicious is the innocent."

"I'm out of that game."

The creature laughed again.

"One you took today. Not fully innocent but enough to bring satisfaction."

"That was necessary. I didn't enjoy it. I regret it. I would have saved him if I could."

"Regrets are nothing. The deed is done. Join us, Jenkins. No more regrets, ever again."

"I've got a boatload of regrets already. You're saying you could take them away?"

"Do you regret what you did in the desert?"

"In the desert, I was doing wet work for a cause I believed in. Some innocents got in the way. I regret that. I especially regret the village, but you made me do that."

"We made you do nothing. Resisting if you wanted to. It's in your blood, Jenkins. In your soul."

"I'm done with that."

"Today you killed already. There are five sleeping around the fire. Repugnant you find them. Souls for the taking. Not innocent, but still delicious. Take them for us. The way you did in the desert. Become one of us."

"I'm not taking any of them unless they get in my way. They're incompetent pigs, but that's all they'll ever be. They're about as dangerous as a bag full of puppies."

"But their souls, Jenkins. Still delicious. We will share,"

"Not interested. Not back in the desert and not now."

The thing took on a harder-edged, slavering voice.

"A born killer, you are, Jenkins. You belong with us. Join or we will take them, one by one, until there is only you. Then we will take you. Not to join, but for your soul. It will not be slow. Only a few days to change your mind."

"I'll think about it," said Jenkins.

"Waste not our time, Jenkins. Clock is ticking."

The thing slithered back into the undergrowth and away. Jenkins took a Coleman lantern and studied the place where the thing had been. There was no sign. Just like in the desert.

***

Jenkins took the van into Portland with the excuse that they needed supplies, which wasn't exactly a lie.

Graham had wanted one of the others to go with him, but Jenkins stared him down again. He said two would be suspicious, and Graham reluctantly agreed.

He drove immediately to the safe house where Jeanine was waiting.

"You stink," she opened with.

"I've been in the woods for five days. What do you expect?"

She ended the formalities.

"A banker was allegedly abducted three days ago, presumably outside a whorehouse he frequented. Late at night. Probably around three or four in the morning. There were no witnesses. He hasn't been heard from since and his family has filed a missing person report. They're taking it seriously. Despite his questionable habits, he is an important man."

"What's that got to do with me?"

"I think it was your cell. None of the more serious outfits truck with relatively penny ante shit like abducting Jewish bankers."

"Mine aren't the only newbies around. They're sprouting up like fungus. Besides, my group of morons couldn't abduct a pig in a poke."

"With your help, they might."

"I'm a deep cover operative. I observe. I didn't observe anything or I'd be reporting it to you right now."

"So you're telling me we could go over the back of that van with a full CSI unit and not find a shred of this man's DNA."

"That's what I'm telling you. Trust me, these guys couldn't abduct a friendly dog, much less a fully grown man, drunk or not."

"Who said he was drunk?"

Jenkins cursed himself. It was that kind of slip that could get him in deep shit.

"I assumed. A man walking out of a whorehouse at four in the morning has to have had more than a few. Liquor flows freely in those kinds of places. Or so I've heard."

Jeanine regarded him silently for a few moments.

"Don't make assumptions. And don't make me suspicious of you. Get these guys wrapped up. It doesn't sound like it'll be too hard."

"Harder than you think. They don't do more than throw around racial slurs and shoot rifles, half-assed I might add, at targets I built for them. If they plan anything serious you'll be the first to know."

"Like abducting a banker."

"Just like that."

"I want to see you back with a report in two weeks. Bring me something. I'm thinking of pulling you."

"Thank God. All I want is off of this shit detail."

"We'll talk about it then. Keep your eyes and ears open. Sometimes the amateurs do something stupid and we can nail them."

"Will do, agent. I've got to pick up supplies and get back before dark."

"Then you best get to it."

***

Jenkins's hands were sweaty on the steering wheel. If Jeanine were to find out he was complicit in the abduction and murder of the banker he would be a dead man. They would never find his body. It was a slip-up, and he couldn't afford it anymore.

He had picked up a two-week supply of MREs, charcoal, lighter fluid, batteries, ammunition, and a case of whiskey. All different shops, all over town. It was dusk by the time he pulled off onto the dirt road that led to the campsite.

"You took long enough," said Graham.

"That's because I'm careful. Unload this shit and let me get some rest."

The others acquiesced while Jenkins sat on a tree stump and field-stripped his carbine. If he needed to shoot any of these assholes he wanted to make sure the gun wouldn't jam.

They broke into the whiskey without bothering to eat. Jenkins expected a rowdy night. Arguments, a couple of fist fights, then the peaceful respite of them all passing out. He would be up all night again, except for dozing. The things were out there. He didn't want to get caught unawares.

He was dozing when the screams started. Immediately awake, he grabbed his carbine and ran toward the sound. The others we slower to respond, still half drunk, but they were shortly behind him.

What they found was Ross, or what was left of him. He had been torn to pieces, dismembered, and gutted. A sturdy branch had been driven into the ground and his head was jammed on top. His face was gashed, but it was obvious he had been conscious for a good part of the attack as what was left of his face was frozen in a rictus of terror and pain.

"What the fuck happened," Green said in barely a whisper.

"Some kind of animal attack," said Graham, attempting to take charge. His face shone pale in the moonlight.

"Get the Colemans. We need to see better than this." Green, and two others, Marsh and Fuchs, headed back to the campsite and returned with two Coleman lanterns. The light did nothing but make the scene more grisly. Fuchs threw up in the bushes.

"What the hell happened?" asked Marsh, "Why was he out of the camp?"

"Must've gone for a piss or something," said Graham. "Then whatever it was got him. Which begs the question. What were you doing that you missed him leaving camp, Jenkins?"

"Sleeping, asshole. I was awake most of the night last night and all day yesterday. You guys are shit for setting and establishing a watch schedule. I drifted off. The screams woke me up. If you nimrods hadn't been half in the bag you would have gotten there as fast as I did."

Another staring contest ensued. Jenkins won again.

"But what could have done this?" Green said in a tremulous voice.

"Some kind of animal. Maybe a bear or a mountain lion," Graham said.

"Mountain lions kill for prey. Bears kill when they're threatened," said Fuchs, getting ahold of himself. "Whatever did this killed for fun. And what kind of wild animal spikes a head on a post like some kind of fucking trophy?"

"What do you have to say, Jenkins? You're quiet," said Graham.

"I don't know. I would say people did this. A group. And they did it fast. Nothing else kills like this."

"We're the only ones out here! We scouted for miles and there was no sign of others. Are you saying they ambushed him, did this, and disappeared in the fifteen minutes it took us to get here?"

"That's what it looks like. I'll scout for tracks. Give me one of the Colemans. "

Jenkins made a show of searching for tracks knowing he wouldn't find anything.

"There's nothing I could find. These people are good."

Graham said, "From now on I want watch three hours long, starting at sundown. If anyone sleeps on the job I'll make what happened to Moss look friendly. Patrols during the day starting at noon. Two-man teams. One in the camp. Jenkins, you're with me north and west. Marsh and Fuchs you take south and east. Green, you watch the camp. We'll rendezvous back at the camp in three hours. That's until we know what or who did this."

Jenkins, of course, knew exactly what did it.

***

At sunrise, the men ate MREs and proceeded to break back into the whiskey. The patrols weren't going to start that day.

"C'mon, Jenkins. Have a slug. Respect for the dead and all that."

Jenkins wiped the top of the bottle, took a drink, and felt it burn down his throat. He avoided coughing. He wasn't a drinker.

"I'm taking a walk," Jenkins announced. "Down to the road and back. I'll look for signs of tracks, although I doubt they came and went that way."

The others didn't seem to care, although Graham gave him a suspicious look.

He walked down the dirt track until he hit the main road five miles down and got cell service on his burner phone. He called Jeanine,

"Attaway," she answered promptly.

"It's Jenkins. Moss is dead. Someone tore him to pieces and mounted his head on a spike. And they did it fast. Fifteen or twenty minutes tops. I looked for tracks but couldn't find any."

"Forgive me if I don't shed a tear."

"Forgive me if I don't."

What's the purpose of this call?"

"You said you wanted updates. I'd call this one motherfucker of an update."

"What happens to the pissants is no concern of mine, unless they turn violent. Just keep Graham alive. I want him for questioning. It turns out he's got ties to some dangerous people."

"I'll do what I can, but no promises. One question", he asked innocently. "Do you have a tactical team out here? They're the only ones who could get Moss and disappear like that,"

"No tactical team. You're on your own. Don't worry about Moss or the others. Just get me Graham alive."

She ended the call.

***

As Jenkins had known, the patrols turned up nothing. Green almost opened fire when they came out of the woods.

"Stand down, Green! It's us!" Graham shouted.

Marsh and Fuchs returned a few minutes later, with nothing to report. They broke into the whiskey again. Jenkins was fed up.

"How do you expect to post three-hour watches when you're all drunk?"

"There's nothing out there, Jenkins. We just scouted out the whole area. We'll start the watches tomorrow night. By the way, you're the sober one here. Why don't you drive into town and get us more to drink? We're running low."

Disgusted, Jenkins climbed into the van. Anything to be away from them for a while.

***

Jenkins stayed up all that night. Exhaustion was creeping up on him but, as he had learned as a soldier, you slept when you got the chance. Not always when you wanted or even needed to. The night stayed peaceful. The men snored in their sleeping bags. The thing came at midnight.

"Do you see, Jenkins?" it hissed. "No avoiding. No hunting. No catching. No seeing. Tomorrow we take another."

"Take them all for all I give a shit. They're worthless and nobody that matters is going to miss them."

"Saving you for last, Jenkins. You have a choice. The pleasures are divine. The pain is indescribable."

"I told you I'd think about it."

"Think not too long. Your time approaches."

It slithered away.

Despite himself, Jenkins fell into a restless sleep.

***

Jenkins woke at dawn. He ate an MRE and then started kicking the others awake.

"What the fuck is this?" Graham muttered. "It's barely sunlight." The others were muttering darkly as well.

"Target practice. It's been three days and none of you come close to qualifying as a marksman. With Moss dead I think it would be a good idea if you learned to shoot those carbines you so proudly lug around."

They climbed out of their sleeping bags, mumbling the whole time. Jenkins gave them time to eat, then said, "Field strip your weapons. You have ten minutes."

With much fumbling and cursing, the men were able to disassemble, clean, and assemble their rifles.

"You were all pathetic last time, but since it was your first I'll give you the benefit of the doubt. You've all hunted game, so you're not incompetent, but you've never been in a situation where people were shooting back at you."

Jenkins had set up wooden targets, vaguely human-shaped and painted red, at one edge of the clearing.

"We'll start at fifty yards. You'll be in the tree line, but in a real firefight, you'd want cover anyway. You all have semi-automatic armalites. Fifteen round clips. Squeeze, don't pull the trigger. Three round bursts. Let's see if you can hit anything."

A word considerably stronger than "disappointed" ran through Jenkin's mind at the result. Some of the targets had taken hits, but far fewer than four men firing fifteen rounds each should have accomplished. From what Jenkins could tell, Graham had done the best, which didn't surprise him.

"I doubt if you could hit a herd of cows at fifty yards based on this. We're doing this every morning and afternoon until you can at least hit the targets instead of shredding the trees behind them. And lay off the fucking whiskey until after drills."

This didn't thrill anybody, but they had the dignity to look chagrined. Except for Graham.

"I hit my targets. You saw," he said.

"I saw you hit your targets more than the others, but you're no marksman. Still, I'll admit, you have more potential than these others."

This seemed to please Graham. He smiled.

"I didn't think you doled out compliments, Jenkins."

"It wasn't a compliment. At best it was a word of encouragement. Don't let it go to your head."

Graham's brow darkened.

"Fuck you, Jenkins. If your attitude doesn't improve there's going to be blood between us before this is all over."

"I look forward to the day," said Jenkins flatly.

***

Jenkins, lying in his sleeping bag wide awake, heard Fuchs go to relieve Marsh at 2 am. Fuchs was still drunk and couldn't find Marsh anywhere on the perimeter. He assumed Marsh had crawled off into the bushes to sleep it off. He took up his position and almost immediately passed out.

Green, Fuchs' replacement, found him like that three hours later. He kicked him awake.

"What the fuck are you doing, man? You heard what Graham said about sleeping on the job."

"Fuck that. There's nobody out here. I don't know who got Moss, but they're long gone by now. By the way, did you happen to see Marsh?"

"Why? What happened?"

"Probably nothing. He wasn't around when I came to relieve him. I figured he crawled off somewhere to sleep it off before I settled down to sleep it off myself."

"Why the fuck didn't you wake us up, you dumbshit?"

"I didn't want to get Marsh in any trouble. Besides, I already said I don't think anything happened to him."

"You've got to get your story straight. I'll back you up. Tell Graham you relieved him and he went back to his sleeping bag. That way you can say he got up and wandered off after that. I don't like this. Especially after what happened to Moss."

"He'll turn up. Graham will knock him around some. Maybe me too. Doesn't matter any. As long as that creep Jenkins doesn't get involved I figure we'll be fine."

"I'll agree with you there. Jenkins gives me the creeps. And Graham is scared of him. I'm afraid of Graham, so that makes me doubly afraid of Jenkins."

"I hear that," said Fuchs." You're the last watch. I'm gonna go turn in. In the morning we'll find Marsh and deal with things then."

Jenkins allowed himself to doze off.

***

Green returned to the camp just as Jenkins was kicking the others awake for target practice. Marsh still hadn't posted.

"What the fuck is going on around here?" Graham growled. "Where was he when you relieved him, Fuchs?"

"On post. Barely conscious but he was there. He stumbled off toward his sleeping bag when I relieved him."

"So where the fuck is he now?"

Jenkins said, "He was drunk. He may have missed the camp and is off somewhere lost in the woods. I suppose we should go look for him."

"I suppose so," Graham said grudgingly. "Fuchs and Green take south and east. Me and Jenkins will take north and west. Meet back in three hours, with or without him, and we'll plan further. A single pistol shot in the air if you find something."

After Fuchs and Green had cleared out, Jenkins told Graham, "Back in the service I was a competent tracker. If he went north or west I should be able to track him. He won't have gotten far without leaving spoor in this underbrush."

"Then carry on, fearless leader. Far be it from me to doubt your abilities."

While Jenkins knew the things would leave no tracks, he thought Marsh would have if he were forced to walk. He started at the lookout post.

"Well at some point he wandered about ten yards into the woods and took a piss, then wandered back. It wasn't long after that that they got him."

"Who got him?"

"Whoever 'they' are. He wasn't on his feet. He was dragged."

"Which direction?"

"Pretty much due north."

"Well, let's get going."

They tracked the drag marks for more than a mile before they found Marsh. He was nailed to a tree by a large metal spike through his chest.

"Well, I guess this rules out wild animals," Jenkins said drily.

Graham didn't say anything. He unholstered his pistol and fired a shot into the air.

***

Fuchs and Green showed up forty-five minutes later. Green was stoic, but Fuchs started losing it.

"What the fuck, man?" he said shakily. "What the fuck is going on? Who's doing this? We're just out here minding our own business."

"We're out here training to help overthrow the government and start a race war. There are plenty of people who might take exception to that," said Jenkins.

"Who? Like Antifa?"

"Antifa are generally non-violent unless they're attacked. They may pick fights but they don't throw the first punch. This is something else. These people have some kind of organizational training. They couldn't be pulling this off unless they did."

"Like who?" Graham said. "The government?"

Jenkins replied, "This isn't government or law enforcement work, in my opinion. If it was they just would have stormed the camp and taken us dead or alive."

"Then what?"

"Some kind of left-wing vigilante group. Must've been out here a while. They're well-coordinated and good at what they do."

"How the hell would they have found us? There are hundreds of square miles of forest. And even then how would they know what we are?" Fuchs asked shakily.

"We haven't exactly made an effort to stay quiet. We've been shooting off semi-automatic rifles. That's enough for them to come and investigate. They may have been watching us for a couple of days. And overhearing words like 'nigger', 'kike', 'spic', and 'raghead' would have given them a pretty good idea of what we're about. If they saw us kill that banker there'll be no doubt in their minds."

"When they saw *you* kill that banker," Green said.

"Don't put that shit on me," Jenkins said, an edge of threat entering his voice for the first time. "You're as guilty of that as all of us. If memory serves, it was your idea in the first place. You knew the man's after-hours schedule."

Green looked at the ground and didn't say anything.

"None of this answers the question of what we're going to do about Marsh. How are we going to get him down? How did they get him up there, for Christ's sake?" said Graham.

"We leave him," Jenkins said. "There's no point in using the rest of the daylight on something that may be impossible."

"You're one cold-blooded motherfucker, Jenkins."

"Maybe so and maybe not. It doesn't matter. There's no realistic way to get him down without cutting the tree down, and I for one don't want to be out in these woods after dark. The camp at least affords some protection. We'll have to sleep in shifts if we can. Two awake, two asleep, and neither of the ones awake out of sight of the other. And around the campfire with the perimeter lit by Colemans."

"Fuck that," said Green. "I'm pulling out. Someone is hunting us and I don't intend to be next."

"Nobody's pulling out," Graham growled at his most menacing. "We're here for a reason, and I'll be God-damned if we don't finish what we started. We can be absorbed into other cells, but only if they think we're worth it. Jenkins is right. Marsh stays where he is. When we get back to camp it's target practice. And If I catch any of you trying to leave I'll kill you myself."

They started back to camp.

***

Target practice went pretty much the way Jenkins suspected. Graham showed improvement, but Green and Fuchs were completely inept. He had them try pistols next. All three did better but better didn't amount to much to Jenkins.

When they broke into the whiskey again Jenkins didn't give a shit. He knew they were walking dead men.

At sundown, Graham built up the fire and said, "Two watches. Me and Jenkins on until one and Green and Fuchs one until seven. Eyes on the other at all times. If the fuckers come back start shooting."

Green and Fuchs stayed up for a while, trading hits off a bottle of whiskey before eventually rolling into their sleeping bags. Within minutes they were snoring.

Jenkins and Graham maintained an uncomfortable silence for some time. Graham continued to take sips off a bottle of whiskey. Finally, Graham said, "You're a hard man, Jenkins. Maybe the hardest I've ever met. And I've met a few. Some veterans. None were like you. What did you do or see in Iraq and Afghanistan that turned you this way?"

"I don't talk about the desert."

"C'mon. You can tell me something."

Jenkins paused for a few minutes.

"The desert is in me. And my mind, my soul is in the desert. This place is hell for me. But I have a job to do here."

"Why don't you sign up for one of those groups? Blackwater or whatever. A man like you, they would take you in a second."

"I'm not a mercenary. I don't kill for money. Those men are scum. Give me a cause, something to kill for, and I'll kill for it."

"Like our cause?"

"I'm having more and more trouble seeing that you have much of a cause at all. At least not a realistic one."

"All revolutions start small, Jenkins. It'll take time, but we will win in the end. I may not live to see it, but I know it's going to happen."

"Do you have a strong stomach, Graham?"

"I like to think so. Why do you ask?"

"Because if things go down the way you think they will, it won't be clean. You'll see and do things you'll want to forget but never will."

"I can take it. I know I can. I was made for this."

"Do you want to know the worst thing I ever saw in the desert? I don't talk about the desert, but for you, I'll do it this once to make a point."

"What was it?" Graham asked, almost breathless.

"It was the battle of Falluja. The enemy was putting up too much of a fight and the higher-ups got sick of it. They distributed white phosphorus grenades, which are illegal under international law. Do you know what white phosphorus does to a person?"

"I've never heard of it."

"It cooks the flesh right off the bone in a matter of minutes. The screams are worse than the smell. Men, women, children. There was no distinction. Falluja fell two days after we started using it. Not that there was much left to fall."

"And you did this? How many grenades did you use? How many people did you kill that way?"

"I didn't keep count. More than a few. Men, women, children. I had nightmares for weeks after that op. That's what I mean, Graham. War, revolution, whatever you want to call it, you don't do it cleanly."

"And now? Do you still have nightmares?"

"Graham, I don't dream at all anymore."

***

Jenkins got Fuchs and Green up for their shift. Both were groggy and stank of whiskey.

"Stay the fuck awake. Eyes on each other. Even if you go to piss. If you hear or see anything, shoot first. We'll figure things out later."

Graham was already asleep. Jenkins got into his sleeping bag and allowed himself to fall asleep. He knew what was likely to happen.

***

Jenkins woke at dawn, as he always did. Graham was still asleep. Green was asleep, curled up into his sleeping bag, snoring. Fuchs, sleeping bag and all, was gone.

Without waking the others, he slipped over to the van and slashed all four tires with his boot knife. He knew what Green and Graham were likely to want to do, and he wasn't going to let it happen. For him, the op wasn't over. He roused the others.

Graham went ballistic. He started hitting Green, with hard blows to the face and body. Green didn't try to dodge or resist. Jenkins got between them.

"Enough!" he shouted. "What's done is done. We need to go find Fuchs."

"What's the fucking point?" slurred Green, spitting out a broken tooth. His nose was broken as well. "We all know he's dead. We should go. Now."

"I'm with Green," said Graham. "It's time we cut our losses. We clear the area. Pack up all our shit. Make sure we don't leave anything behind. Make sure there's nothing to connect us to those bodies if they're ever found. Get our asses back to Portland. Ditch the van. Set it on fucking fire. No evidence."

"The van isn't going anywhere," Jenkins said nonchalantly. "They slashed the tires."

"Then we pile everything into the van and torch it here. We walk out. The road is only five miles away."

"You're not thinking, Graham," said Jenkins. "That's an old logging road. Most of the traffic on it is people who are lost or people who want to be lost. Even if someone did stop for us what's our story? Three guys in stained fatigues trying to hitch a ride? Seems like a whole parade of red flags to me. And walking out? Portland is a hundred miles away. Stopping in any small town to get a motel room or even eat at a Wendy's is going to parade those red flags. We'll get picked up for sure. And I don't think either of you will stand up to interrogation. They'll link us to the bodies and we've got no proof to give them otherwise."

"We could hang the whole thing on you," Graham said quietly. "Even the banker."

"You could try, but don't forget I'm trained for this kind of thing. Before it's over you two will be sucking gas in a green room while I'm watching from the other side of the glass."

There was a long, uncomfortable silence while Graham stared at Jenkins and Green stared at Graham. Jenkins stared back. Jenkins had always given Graham the creeps, but now there was something different about him. Something sinister.

"So what do we do?" Graham finally asked.

"We find Fuchs. Then we eat, you two get drunk and pass out, and I stay awake all fucking night again watching your sorry asses. In the morning I'll walk to the road. I've got a burner phone I didn't tell you about. If I can get a signal there are people I can call to bring us in."

"You had a phone this whole time? What the fuck, Jenkins? That was rule number one! No phones! They can track phones!"

"I bought it at Walmart. Prepaid. No record. But fuck you and your indignation. I didn't know any of you and didn't trust any of you. I could hardly come out into the cold without backup. It's all beside the point now. We find Fuchs. We walk to the road tomorrow. I call in the cavalry. It's not happening any other way."

Graham went for his sidearm. Jenkins was faster.

"Drop it, Graham. I'll put you down without thinking about it. Green, pull yours and toss it over to my feet. Don't think for a second I can't take both of you before either of you can get off a shot."

Graham let his pistol fall to the ground. Green unholstered his and tossed it over.

"Okay. Now the two of you find all the firearms in the camp and put them in the back of the van. All of them. Don't try and hide one. If I see that it'll go worse for you than you think. Then your knives."

"You're leaving us out here with nothing to defend ourselves with!" snarled Graham.

"You've got me. Believe me, I'm better at protecting you from anything that comes along than you could yourselves."

"Like you did the others?"

"As far as I'm concerned they did that to themselves."

Green and Graham spent the next half hour gathering all the guns and putting them in the back of the van. Jenkins watched carefully. When they were done he locked it and put the key in a pocket.

"So what now?"

"What I've been saying. We find Fuchs."

***

Jenkins walked behind the two of them into the woods.

"Just follow the trail of the dragged sleeping bag," he said. "Not even the two of you can miss it."

They trudged on for some time. The forest thinned out a little bit. Suddenly Green leapt off of the trail they were following and went crashing through the underbrush. Graham and Jenkins stopped and listened to him getting farther and farther away until they couldn't hear him anymore.

"Why didn't you shoot him?" Graham asked. "What if he makes it to the road?"

"He won't make it to the road."

"How do you know?"

"I just know. Let's get moving."

***

They found the sleeping bag a half hour later. Above it, nailed to a tree, was a hand. The fingers were curled up except for the index finger, which pointed off into the woods to their right.

"What the fuck do we do now?" said Graham.

"I think that should be obvious. They're leaving us directions."

They set off to the right, following the direction that the finger pointed. About two hundred yards later they found the other hand, manipulated in the same way as the other. It pointed off about forty-five degrees to their left. They set off in that direction. Some time later they found a booted foot, placed on the ground in such a way as to lead them off in a new direction still. The same thing with the other foot.

When they found Fuchs' head on a ragged tree stump, eyes and mouth sewn shut with thick twine, Graham said, "Enough of this shit. I'd say we've found enough of Fuchs to know there's no point in finding the rest of him."

"For once I agree with you. If we start back now we can make the camp before sundown."

"How the hell are we going to find the camp? We're completely lost."

"You keep forgetting who I am, Graham. You may be lost, but I'm not. Just stay close behind me and we'll make the clearing in a little over an hour, by my estimate. And keep it in the front of your thoughts that if you try and take me from behind, I'll snap your fucking neck."

***

They made the camp an hour and a half later. The sun was westering, already below the tree line.

"Get the fire going, Graham. Then sit your ass down and start drinking."

"What are you going to do?"

I'm having dinner. Then I'm going to sit here with you."

"I'm hungry. Why don't you let me have something to eat?"

"You'll live. Get the fire going."

Graham got the fire lit and built up as Jenkins ate an MRE. Then he pulled a fifth of whiskey out of the box and cracked the seal. He took a long pull.

"So, when do we walk to the road and call in your people?" he said.

"I haven't decided. Not until after Green posts, at least."

"I thought you said we wouldn't see him again."

"I didn't say that at all. I said he wouldn't make the road, and he won't. We'll see him again. Probably tonight if I'm not fucked up about the timing."

"What are you talking about?"

"Maybe I'll tell you tomorrow if I decide you deserve to know."

"Who the fuck are you, really, Jenkins?"

"Well, let's start simple. I'm a veteran of two ugly foreign wars, which I mostly enjoyed the fuck out of. The people who make decisions like this decided I enjoyed it too much, so they made me quit. When I got back States-side the DOJ recruited me to infiltrate your pathetic little group. So, for a while at least, I worked for the government. But I don't think I do anymore."

"You son of a bitch. I knew from the start there was something off about you. I should have trusted my instincts."

"There's something off about me, Graham, but it doesn't have anything to do with me being a DOJ asset. Maybe I'll tell you about it before our time runs out. I will say this – you definitely should have trusted your instincts."

They sat silently for a while. An owl hooted off in the distance. Graham started feeling the whiskey.

"What do you mean, 'before our time runs out'?"

"I haven't decided yet," said Jenkins. "All I can tell you right now is that you maybe, just maybe, might live through this. I'll make up my mind after Green posts."

"So you might kill us both."

"Or neither of you, which you might live long enough to regret."

"I have no idea what you're talking about."

"One way or another, you'll find out. Shut up and drink your whiskey."

***

Around midnight Graham was starting to nod off. He slowly became aware of a sound. A faint, mewling kind of moan. The sound an animal in agony might make. He ignored it for a while but came to realize it was steadily getting louder, and closer. It didn't sober him up, but it brought him around.

"What the fuck is that noise?" he said.

"That'll be Green, I expect. Let's go check it out. You just stagger on in front of me and follow your ears. Take a Coleman."

It didn't take long to find Green. He was about thirty yards out of the clearing. His legs had been cut off at the knees, his arms at the elbow. He was crawling slowly forward on what was left of his limbs.

"Jesus Christ, Green! What the fuck happened to you?"

As he spoke, Graham noticed the blood running down Green's chin and realized that his tongue had been cut out. He continued to crawl forward, making the ghastly mewling noise. His eyes were a cry for relief. Or release.

Jenkins stepped around Graham and shot Green in the head.

***

The next morning Graham awoke around noon with a pounding headache, feeling weak and dehydrated. Jenkins sat cross-legged across the fire pit, awake and alert, pistol in his lap.

"Can I get some water?" Graham croaked.

"Knock yourself out."

Graham got up and went to the supply pile and got himself a bottle of water. He went back and sat down and sucked down half of it, which made him feel bloated and sick.

Finally, he said, "What the fuck did we see last night?"

"They've upped the game," Jenkins replied. "They knew I'd kill him, which is why they didn't kill him themselves. Like they did the others."

"Jesus, Jenkins. Who the fuck are you talking about?"

"Well, since things seem to have come to a head, I'll tell you a little about it. You need to imagine evil. Evil as an active force. Something self-aware and working toward evil purposes, whatever that means. Can you imagine such a thing, Graham?"

"Yeah, I guess so."

"Now I need you to imagine something darker than that. Something maybe even more powerful. Something so dark it feeds on evil, as well as good and everything else you can imagine. Can you imagine such a thing, Graham?"

"I don't understand what the fuck you're getting at."

"Well, whatever I decide, you'll understand tonight. I'll tell you this. You're not getting out alive. The only difference is whether you get a clean death or a dirty one. I think I'm going to duct tape you up now. I don't have time for desperate last measures."

***

Twilight fell. Jenkins built up the fire, then sat down and waited. Graham whimpered behind the duct tape.

The stars came out. There was a slithering, slavering sound in the woods, loud and clear. Jenkins got up and dragged Graham to the edge of the clearing, setting him up on his knees. There was a presence, or many presences, writhing just outside the firelight. Long, sharp teeth reflected red in the glow. A voice came from the writhing mass, chilling Graham to the bone. He was too terrified to even whimper.

"Time has come, Jenkins. Decision have you made?"

Jenkins said, "Why did you make me kill Green? Why didn't you do him yourselves, like the others?"

"Deciding yourself, Jenkins. Mercy. Not liking mercy. What of the worm beside you, all taped up? Time is up, Jenkins. Decide."

"There's one thing left. If I come with you, if I join with you, we go back to the desert. If we're not going to the desert, you can have my soul for dinner, no matter the pain."

Amidst the liquid sound of the slithering and slavering a susurrus arose, as though a discussion was being had. It didn't last long.

Finally, the voice said, "This we agree to, Jenkins. Desert is delicious. Always much to eat in the desert. Join us."

"Then I give you this soul."

Jenkins shot Graham in the head. He dropped the gun, spread his arms, and walked into the bosom of darkness.

***

A jogger found him in a clearing. There was a gray van, the remains of a campfire, and several discarded MREs. She jogged back to the logging road and called the police. He was identified as Captain Paul Jenkins of The United States Marine Corps who had done two tours of duty in Iraq and two in Afghanistan. A decorated soldier who had been given a section eight discharge due to increasingly erratic behavior. After stepping off a transport plane at Nellis Air Force Base three weeks earlier he had promptly disappeared.

Captain Jenkins was suffering from exposure and was catatonic. It was estimated that he had been in the woods for roughly two weeks. His condition suggested that he had been in his current state for at least two or three days. He was airlifted to a Portland hospital where military psychologists attempted to debrief him, but he never became responsive. The only evidence that there was someone in there was a slight, enigmatic smile that never left his face.

The authorities found no evidence that there had been anyone with him in the woods.

THE RESURRECTIONIST
Zach Ellenberger

    The tale for which I am about to tell is often merited as nothing more than petty urban legends. Most local townsfolk accustomed to the story of poor Edmund Raye are quick to discredit such tall tales of what they would consider delusional grandeur. It exists today as nothing more than a mere ghost story to frighten children. But for those contemporaries of Mr. Raye in the small town of Barrington, Pennsylvania, the tale of his horrific fate was far too real. Despite what speculation may arise in direct conflict with one's resolve to the truth of such matters, the circumstances surrounding the peculiar Edmund Raye remain a mystery. Those who do well to exercise common sense know there was indeed something unconscionable at the heart of Barrington.
    Dark were the days of yore for the small town nestled deep in the ancient mountains of Appalachia where

superstitions ran rampant. Rumors abound that the town of Barrington had been cast in darkness since the early days of the country's founding, contributed to a curse brought upon by natives who had been driven from their homes. Shadowed by the outbreak of cholera in the 1850s, the town had become isolated and cut off from the rest of society. The few travelers who occasionally passed through the grim town kept their visits brief and often whispered of evil creatures lurking in the deepest corners of the surrounding forests. The locals grew intimate with the cold grip of death through disease and the alleged hauntings of forest spirits like the Wendigo, a flesh-eating monster of native myth. Though many believed the disappearance of several children to be the work of evil forces, Edmund did not partake in such rumors and hysteria.

  Edmund was a graveyard watchman at the Lord's Haven Parish. An old hermit, Edmund grew up in Barrington spending much of his childhood in the silent cemetery where he claimed he could commune with the dead. Edmund's farcical assertions drew much scrutiny from the townsfolk as well as resentment from his own family. The cause of his parents' deaths was a mystery in and of itself to which the town speculated young Edmund as the cause, suspecting the boy to have brought a curse upon his parents from his frequent visits to the graveyard. With no other family willing to care for him, the church took the boy under its wing and raised him, giving him access to the graveyard at any time of the day. Seeing the boy's affinity to spend his time with the dead, the parishioner offered him a job as the cemetery watchman once Edmund came of age, which he gladly accepted. Edmund remained in that role ever since.

Edmund kept to himself as he grew older into adulthood, eventually reaching a ripe old age when cholera reared its ugly face in Barrington killing half the town's population. Edmund's tale began shortly after the outbreak. It was during the harvest of 1855 with the death of Mayor George Caulfield's fifteen-year-old daughter, Annie Mae Caulfield. The cause of death, as declared by Dr. Newton Penn of the local medical institute, was another case of cholera. Her death had struck the town heavily as it was the first case of cholera in six months since the outbreak struck. In the early morning of a grey autumn day, a collective of townsfolk gathered in the Lord's Haven cemetery to pay their respects and lay the young and beautiful Annie Mae to eternal rest. Edmund was present as part of his duties as cemetery watchman to lower the casket and fill the burial plot. The Caulfields were reluctant to accept their daughter's death, the fairest maiden throughout the town. Although Dr. Penn had declared the young girl dead, Mayor Caulfield and his wife, Cynthia, clung to every thread of hope that it wasn't true. At the behest of his distraught wife, George arranged for Annie Mae to be buried in a safety coffin fitted with a bell. That way, if there was any chance that Annie Mae still lived, she could signal them. George, wanting nothing more than to console his wife, obliged her despite the doctor's best efforts to convince them otherwise.

"I cannot imagine the pain you are enduring in these difficult times," Dr. Penn empathized at her burial. "I understand that it takes time to accept such hard truths and let go, but you must take solace in knowing that she is in the hands of God. If there's anything you need, please don't hesitate to ask."

Dr. Penn was a cordial man indeed in the face of sorrow. He was tall and handsome, a desirable bachelor to the available women of Barrington. He was well respected around town as well as in the medical field for his work in the prognosis of diseases. Yet, the man paraded around town as if the threat of death had no consequence for him. Before he left the cemetery, he approached Edmund speaking to him quietly out of earshot of the Caulfields.

"Tonight, at the stroke of midnight."

Edmund nodded silently and returned to his duties. The Parishioner, Father Campbell, gave a final blessing over the body and then offered his condolences to Mr. And Mrs. Caulfield before returning to the confines of the parish. George and Cynthia remained at the side of Annie Mae's grave until Edmund finished lowering the coffin. They spoke their final farewells and departed the cemetery to begin their life without their beloved daughter.

The midnight hour was fast approaching, and a heavy fog fell over the cemetery grounds that night. The silence was palpable. As Edmund waited for the stroke of midnight per Dr. Penn's instructions, he decided to patrol the yard to ensure everything was in order. Edmund walked amongst the tombstones as he did time and time before. With his nightly perusal of the grounds, he came to memorize the names of all that lay within the confines of the cemetery. Though dead they may have been, they were still very much alive in

Edmund's mind. He would carry on conversations with nothing but the tombstones to help pass the time. It was a most remarkable thing, he thought to himself – this fascination with the finality of death. One's greatest folly was the refusal to accept death as part of life. For Edmund, there was no greater companionship than humans' dance with death, for the dead did not trouble themselves with the concerns of the living.

As he wandered deeper into the dark of night, his senses had been awoken by a strange noise carrying upon the air. He stopped and perked his ears. What he heard in that moment was undeniably the sound of voices echoing in the distance.

"Have I been so pensive as to have lost track of the time?" he thought aloud, assuming Dr. Penn had arrived and found his way into the cemetery. But it occurred to Edmund that he could not pinpoint the source of the voices as they seemed to have encircled him like the wind. He turned and started for the gate of the cemetery when the voices began to grow louder. As they grew louder, Edmund could feel his heart begin to pulse heavily, filling him with anxiety. It became clear that the voices were not of this world, for they chanted in unison speaking a language unbeknownst to Edmund that instilled such fear in him he refused to press on. He stopped dead in his tracks. With his lantern in hand, he turned about in place searching for the voices which now seemed so near to him. In his frenzied state, his eye caught a glimpse of a silhouette lurking on the edge of the darkness. The figure glided in and out of eyesight draped in a pale white dress. Edmund felt a chill reach up his spine. He began to shake uncontrollably as the still of the midnight air crept over him like a shroud.

Suddenly, the strike of a bell rang out, startling Edmund right out of his skin. It was not the bell to which Edmund was expecting – having been waiting for the church bell to toll for the midnight hour – but the echo of a grave's bell! Someone had been buried alive! Edmund hurried off in the direction of the bell's ring. With his lantern outstretched, he searched desperately among the tombstones for the source of the ring. For a moment, the ringing paused. Edmund listened intently.

"I hear you! I hear you! Where are you?"

After a brief moment of silence, the ringing continued. Edmund took off once more. He was almost upon the source when the ringing stopped once again. Before him stood the very grave that he dug earlier that day. It was the grave of young Annie Mae Caulfield. Holding up his lantern to the tombstone, he could see the bell swaying softly back and forth as if it had just been ringing!

It was then that he felt a hand grab his shoulder out of nowhere. Edmund shrieked and, wrenching his shoulder free, fell to the ground losing grasp of his lantern. He crawled away in terror. Working up the courage, he looked back and there stood Dr. Penn with two of his handlers, known only as Vincent and Malcolm. Dr. Penn bore a look of confusion while Edmund squirmed on the ground steeped in his bewilderment.

"By God, what has gotten into you, Edmund? What is going on?"

"She is alive!"

"Who?"

"Annie Mae! She is alive! Her bell was ringing." The doctor tried to calm Edmund down, but he was far too hysterical.

"There's no bell ringing, Edmund. Surely, you must be imagining things."

"By God, I tell you that it was ringing. I was waiting for you when I heard it. Did you not hear it? She lives!"

The three men stared at Edmund suspiciously. The two handlers with Dr. Penn, who had already been equipped with shovels, began digging. They tore through the dirt with all haste as Edmund and Dr. Penn watched anxiously when they finally struck the wood of the coffin's lid. Edmund feared it was too late for the poor girl and that she had suffocated while waiting for her rescue. The two men pried open the coffin lid.

Alas, to everyone's surprise and confusion, the coffin was empty! No trace of young Annie Mae's remains. Edmund let out a haunting shrill as he stumbled back. Could the figure he potentially saw earlier have been that of Annie Mae?

Dr. Penn did not seem convinced by Edmund's claim. His confusion turned to anger which he directed at Edmund.

"Do you take me for a fool, Raye? I've been paying you good money for a year now to exhume the bodies here for my medical research. I told you earlier today that I need this body for further studies and now, by some miraculous act of God, she turns up missing. Did you think I would not find this suspicious? I will not be undermined by the likes of you, Raye!"

"The same soil lay at your feet as mine. You saw yourself, that ground remained unbroken since I last filled it earlier this day. How could I have removed the body beforehand? And whom do you reckon would I have sold it to, other than you?" Edmund pleaded with the doctor, insisting that Dr. Penn believe his story.

"Well Raye, it could not have just stood up and walked out of the graveyard. You have until tomorrow night to produce the body, or you can be certain our deal is off! Then I will have a mind to claim you for my research."

Dr. Penn stormed off with his two handlers leaving Edmund to refill the grave by himself. Edmund remained on the ground watching Dr. Penn disappear into the heavy fog. For the first time in his life, Edmund felt fear of being left alone in the graveyard.

Edmund sat inside the watchman's shack within the cemetery grounds trying to calm himself with a flask full of potato brandy. There was to be no sleep for Edmund Raye that fateful night. A few hours had passed since his alleged witnessing of ghostly apparitions. Edmund replayed the moment over and over again in his head – the coffin lid opening to reveal nobody inside. What could have possibly happened to Annie Mae's body? Edmund was the only soul in the cemetery since Annie Mae's burial, so it could not have been possible for someone to have removed it without Edmund's knowledge. He had hoped the brandy would wake him up from this dreadful nightmare. Much to his dismay, it only made the ordeal more real. Edmund contemplated the circumstances: If word had gotten out among the town that Annie Mae's body had gone missing, they would have rightfully blamed Edmund and it would surely have led to Edmund's hanging. Edmund did not have much reason to suspect Dr. Penn would say anything, for it would only lead to his demise as well. However, Edmund could not speak to the legitimacy and motives of Dr. Penn's two handlers, Victor and Malcolm. What if they had plans to extort both Edmund and Dr. Penn for their gain? What if they were the ones who stole Annie Mae's body? But how? Edmund's mind continued to race with consequence. Growing even more anxious, he swigged more brandy.

Edmund sat in silence waiting restlessly for the break of dawn while the wind howled in the distance. The night had grown uncomfortably calm for Edmund. He spoke softly to himself to help shake his discomfort.

"A despicable night, indeed. I must resolve this absurdity and make amends with my sanity. What nonsense have I let myself succumb to? The dead do not trouble themselves with the concerns of the living. Come the dawn, I shall be vindicated."

It was no sooner he finished his thought when he began to hear the voices in the air slowly begin to chant. Edmund tensed up and perked his ears toward the night. This time, the chanting was accompanied by the faint laughter of a child. Peering out of the shack, Edmund held up his lantern and gazed out into the dark of night dimly lit by the light of the moon. Suddenly, on the edge of his periphery through the thick fog appeared the whitened silhouette Edmund saw earlier that night. His heart began to race at the sight but tempered himself with invigorating words.

"There it appears again, the elusive wretch; a prank, I would conclude, and nothing more. And yet why does it choose to torment me on this night of all nights? What kind of hell has embraced this place? I must embolden myself and prove that my sanity still reigns supreme. The dead do not trouble themselves with the concerns of the living. Come the dawn, I shall be vindicated!"

Edmund stepped out once more into the night in pursuit of the silhouette, determined to prove once and for all that his imagination had no authority over his reality. He moved quickly in the direction of the apparition, convinced of his misguided sanity. But, for as much ground as he covered, the figure managed to stay the same distance from Edmund, just upon the edge of his sight. Edmund felt his frustration begin to get the better of him as he picked up speed. The quicker he moved, the louder the chanting voices grew. Eventually, the chanting gradually drowned out the child's laughter, distorting it to the point of resembling blood-curdling screams. Edmund's frustration turned to fear as he felt the voices growing closer as if they were creeping up on him. He stopped dead in his path to catch his breath when he looked down and took notice of one of the tombstones near his feet. The tombstone was completely blank. This perturbed Edmund for he knew with great certainty that there was not a single tombstone in the cemetery without a name and date of departure. He looked closely at the tombstone rubbing his fingers along it. Sure enough, no etchings had ever grazed the surface of this tombstone. He looked at the tombstones to the right and the left; both of them were blank as well. It was at this moment Edmund realized that the apparition faded out of sight. But what was more concerning to him was that all the tombstones were now blank. In realizing this, he felt the ground begin to shudder at his feet and a loud crash filled the night like the sound of thunder. It was an unnatural roar as if it came from the very depths of Hell. Then, after a moment of silence, the jingle of a bell began ringing out once more in the dead of night. There was no mistaking it; it was the very same bell he heard only hours earlier!

He hurried after the bell once more. Rushing through the dark with nothing but his lantern, the chanting turned to hisses like snakes closing in from all around. He arrived at the tomb of young Annie Mae Caulfield. A single beam of moonlight broke through the foggy dark illuminating the ground around her grave. The earth had been churned up and the coffin protruded from beneath. It had not been the work of a shovel but rather seemed as if the coffin was forced out of the ground by the Earth itself. Edmund could see that the lid of the coffin was once again removed, and nobody lingered within.

That was all that Edmund could tolerate. He had been pushed far beyond his wits and chose to rid himself of such delusions. He turned to make his way toward the gate when – to his horror – was confronted face to face with the hideous silhouette he had been chasing all night. He cried out in frightful horror. In his shock, he realized the silhouette was that of Annie Mae Caulfield, withered and decrepit. Her hair resembled cobwebs, her skin broken and cold to the touch. Her sunken pitch-black eyes – empty and soulless – were a source of tremendous and overwhelming fear unbeknownst to Edmund, instilling within him an unforgiving sense of dread and trepidation. The entire length of Edmund's back seized up, gripped by the cold embrace of fear as he fell helplessly to the ground. He struggled to look away but could not break his gaze which had been fixated upon her hideous face. She then pounced upon him like a spider, pinning him against the very grave in which she once resided. He pleaded desperately for his life.

"Spirit, I beseech thee! Have mercy. I'm but a simple watchman and I've no desire to perturb you. I am merely tasked with tending to the deceased."

Then, the spirit spoke like that of a hundred voices in one.

"Dweller cursed be you still! For you do not stand free of consequence and must answer for your sins against innocent flesh."

"Great spirit, you mistaken me. I've done no ill will against those living or dead. What is it that compels you to torment me? The dead do not trouble themselves with the concerns of the living!"

"But the living troubles themselves with concern for the dead. They fear fate, and yet, fate is inevitable no matter what they do. Lest they forget, death is the final form for all."

"Then, why has thou come for me?"

"You have desecrated the remains of those who reside within this sacred ground. You have laid your hands upon blessed souls since passed on and sold their remains to hollow men for your gain. Now, their souls may never rest."

Edmund began to weep uncontrollably, begging for his life.

"Please, it is not as you say. I only did so for the good of the town. Death has run rampant here in Barrington. These deaths have been attributed to nothing more than disease. It was only my intention to assist Dr. Penn who has worked to develop a cure for the sick. You see, I was trying to save them!"

"The less you know, Resurrector. You fail to recognize the doctor's true intentions. The doctor is the reason the disease has returned to Barrington. He has been going about town infecting innocent lives with formulated doses of the cholera disease. Once he collects their bodies, they become his puppets to do with as he pleases."

Edmund could not begin to comprehend the apparition's claim.

"That can't be possible," Edmund protested. "Dr. Penn has been well-favored among the townsfolk for years."

"Then perhaps you are the fool the doctor claims you to be. Either way, I will have my due."

"But I am not ready to die."

"Your death will come in time. But not tonight. For now, you serve a more important purpose."

"What purpose is that, pray tell?" Edmund insisted.

"Every corpse you have resurrected represents a soul that has been unaccounted for, a body desecrated by the blasphemous hands of Dr. Penn. Therefore, an imbalance exists in nature. I demand what I am owed, and I will have it. I require seven souls. If you wish for this torment to end, deliver these seven souls before the stroke of midnight tomorrow. Only then will your torment cease."

"I shall do as I am bid. Of whom do you seek?"

Without answering, the ghost of Annie Mae curled back her lips, revealing razor-sharp fangs like that of a wild animal, and, lurching onto Edmund, sunk them into Edmund's neck. Startled, Edmund struggled to free himself from her grip to no avail. His sight faded to white as he felt the pain shoot from his neck throughout his body. The same cold embrace seized his entire body this time, causing him to twitch and squirm uncontrollably. Thinking himself dead, he stopped resisting and let himself succumb to the pain. Suddenly, the white light faded, and the pain vanished as Edmund regained consciousness. He found himself in the center of town far from the cemetery. How he got there, or what time of the night it was, he could not be sure. The ghost of Annie Mae was nowhere in sight nor was any living soul. Edmund climbed to his feet when he noticed something troubling. His vision remained hazy, and his body went numb. And yet, he was still moving, walking in the direction of Dr. Penn's lab. Edmund grew distressed, for it was as if he had no control over his body and was being led by someone or something else. He fought his movements at every turn, unable to change his course.

By God, I must be possessed! he thought to himself as he hobbled down the street towards Dr. Penn's medical institute resembling that of a cripple. Suddenly, the disembodied voice of the apparition – that of a hundred voices in one – spoke to Edmund, as if it were Edmund himself speaking.

"The balance between worlds must be maintained. A debt is owed, to be paid only in blood. The first souls are those of Dr. Penn and his handlers, Vincent and Malcolm. For years, the doctor and his handlers have preyed upon the townsfolk for their gain. He is a defiler of flesh and life and his henchmen remain blind by greed, paid to hold their tongues, monsters of inherent chaos, abominations to the sanctity of human life. They must be eradicated."

Edmund approached Dr. Penn's lab, a puppet under the control of the vile apparition. He was led to a door at the rear of the building, isolated from the view of the streets. Edmund yanked at the door handle to find that it was locked. He then heard the sound of a light click and the door silently swung open. The door led into a storage room packed to the brim with experimental medical equipment and devices that had been previously rendered obsolete. The shelves within the storage room were stacked with tools and notebooks full of medical notations as well as the discarded bones of humans and beasts alike. They created a maze-like labyrinth which led to a pair of double doors. Edmund stepped through the double doors and found himself in the medical auditorium. Here, Dr. Penn's peers would gather and bear witness to his latest atrocity, claiming it to be the work of a medical genius.

Edmund came upon one of Dr. Penn's handlers, Vincent, who was fast asleep in one of the pews. Edmund felt his heartbeat race as he approached the sleeping man. Vincent was a scraggly man with an unkempt beard and wiry frame. Standing over the man, Edmund fell short of breath and began to panic. He tried to remain standing so as not to wake Vincent, but his entire body went limp as a cloud of fog began to fill the room. Vincent was awakened by Edmund's body falling to the ground, startled and confused as to how Edmund got inside. Edmund remained weak and helpless. Thinking he had failed his task, he forfeited himself to Vincent. But as Vincent reached for Edmund, the ghostly apparition of Annie Mae appeared from the cloud of fog behind Vincent. Stunned and shocked, Edmund watched the apparition seize Vincent by the throat and proceeded to tear out Vincent's eyes, ears, and tongue. Vincent cried out in unimaginable pain and agony but eventually died on the spot.

His screams alerted the second handler, Malcolm, to Edmund's presence. Malcolm rushed into the auditorium only to find Edmund lying next to Vincent's dead body. Malcolm was twice the size of Edmund and much taller, drenched in sweat from exerting even the simplest amount of energy. His clean-shaven face bore a look of disgust as his gaze wandered back and forth between Edmund and Vincent. The look transfigured into anger as he marched toward

Edmund. But the apparition appeared before him, snatching his tongue from his mouth and ripping out his eyes and ears as well. Before Malcolm could realize what had been done to him, fell to the ground, asphyxiated by his blood. Both men were dead in a matter of minutes. The apparition looked toward Edmund with her blackened eyes before disappearing once more. As soon as she did, Edmund regained his strength and continued. In the back of the auditorium was the door to Dr. Penn's chambers where he resided.

The room was dimly lit by candles as Edmund snuck through the door. What he witnessed on the other side of the door was a dungeon of horrors far surpassing anyone's imagination. Along the walls, there hung what looked like sheets of flayed human skin, boiled and treated. There were anatomical sketches of humans and beasts alike, both skeletal as well as muscular structures. Between the sketches were aged stains of blood coated all over the place. But, at the center of the room lay the butchered bodies of Dr. Penn's lab experiments. The bodies were surgically opened and drained of their blood. Though difficult to recognize, Edmund knew they were the deceased townsfolk that he had sold to the doctor, now nothing more than playthings for Dr. Penn's twisted machinations.

A man stood before the far wall of the room which displayed what could best be described as a shrine comprised of human and animal body parts. The beastly shrine had taken the form of the monstrous Wendigo. Edmund recalled the legend of the Wendigo which still circulated amongst the town with those close in trade with the local natives. Some say Barrington was cursed at its founding by the tribal chief in response to the atrocities committed by the colonists against the natives which only caused further tensions between the two cultures. Legend has it that that chief's curse summoned dark, vengeful spirits such as the wendigo among others to prey upon the land and its new inhabitants. Now it seemed as though the legend had come to life.

The hybrid body had been fastened to the wall with wood and nails. The arms and torso carried signs of human origin while the legs were hooves and the head was adorned with a large animal skull fitted with antlers. The flesh that clung to the bones was pale and discolored. The discoloration had been brought about by syringes filled with a peculiar, discolored serum. The man standing before the shrine was hunkered over the table examining the liquid within the syringes. His once white apron had been heavily stained with blood

The man turned to Edmund, who had been standing directly behind him now. It was none other than Dr. Penn. He had a sinister, twisted look in his eyes; his face was pale, gaunt, and coated in blood.

"Edmund? You dare enter my lab without permission? You are not welcome in this place!"

Edmund was incensed with uncontrollable ire. The doctor had been the source of all his suffering at the hands of the apparition. Edmund would not dare to let this opportunity pass.

"She was never sick, was she? None of them were before you put your cursed hands upon them."

"You know nothing of the darkness that curses these lands," Dr. Penn hissed. "The great spirit has lurked among the town's periphery for years plaguing it with disease and famine. The only way to survive is to appease it. It has chosen me to herald its arrival. Yes, I am the bridge between worlds, the conduit between spiritual and physical. I am its harbinger, and it demands sacrifices in flesh and blood to be fulfilled."

Edmund could no longer contain his anger. Never had Edmund desired to take the life of another, but Edmund could not stop himself from killing Dr. Penn. He seized a stray syringe of the serum from the table and stabbed Dr. Penn in the neck, dispatching the green liquid into him. His anger was such that he repeatedly stabbed the doctor. As Edmund regained his senses, he could see the doctor's skin turn jaundiced and blotchy as the veins in his head bulged. The whites of his eyes turned red, and the doctor began foaming at the mouth, choking violently. Whatever Edmund had injected the doctor with had accelerated the decay of his insides as his body shriveled and turned ill. By the time the doctor was dead, his body resembled those of his tortured victims. Upon the doctor's death, another crash of what seemed like thunder filled the air shaking the entire building violently. It was a piercing sound that caused the shrine's skull to fall from the structure, shattering the syringes below.

Edmund could feel his heart still racing as he once again faded out of consciousness. It felt as if he had begun floating upon a sea of calm, bathed in the white light, weightless and horizontal. It did not last long, for once again he regained his consciousness only to find himself back outside the Lord's Haven Parish standing in the entrance to the cemetery. The ghost appeared once more before Edmund, startling him yet again.

"I stand before you, pleading mercy," Edmund begged. "I am not a man of violence. I beg you, make swift work of me so that I may peacefully continue with this dreadful life."

"Your trial is only halfway complete. The next souls I require are that of the parishioner, Father Campbell as well as George and Cynthia Caulfield."

This time, Edmund protested the apparition's instructions.

"Why? Why, tainted spirit, do you find it necessary to take these good people and condemn further innocence?"

"The less you know, Resurrector. The souls you deem to be innocent are far from such. What they do behind closed doors does not escape my sight. Father Campbell disguises himself as a godly man while concealing his true identity as a violator of young children. For years, the priest has preyed upon the children of this town to satiate his perversion of lust. Annie Mae Caulfield was one of the priest's victims, the latest in a sequence of debauchery to which the town remains incognizant."

Edmund could not believe what he had heard; he didn't want to.

"That can't be. A man of God, he is. And what reasons do her parents have to suffer?"

"George and Cynthia Caulfield's sin is one of ignorance toward their daughter. Annie Mae's beauty was incomparable, apt to catch the attention of any man. This was cause for concern among George and Cynthia. Fearing the attraction of undesirable suitors and wanting to protect her from any harm or danger, George and Cynthia left her under the supervision of Father Campbell and the parish to better learn the ways of God. After Father Campbell defiled her, Annie Mae approached her parents about it. But they would not believe her. They refused to believe that a man of the cloth would commit such cruelty against a child. So, she was sent back to the parish day after day under the priest's care. Eventually, Annie Mae refused to go back. Once a sweet, kind girl, her behavior grew erratic and prone to sudden outbursts of aggression. George and Cynthia took her refusal to return to church as a sign of her denouncing God. Suspecting a decline in her mental health, they sent her to Dr. Penn. But Dr. Penn had his plans for the young Annie Mae. Betraying the Caulfield's trust, Dr. Penn tended to young Annie Mae, using the opportunity to inject her with a syringe of the formulated Cholera leading to her death."

The story had at last been fully revealed to Edmund. Its veil had finally been lifted to reveal the quaint little town he had come to know as the scourge and abomination that it truly was. The revelation had conjured a sickening taste in his mouth, one of disgust and repulsion for the human condition. He no longer harbored fear and apprehension for his well-being, but only interminable anger and contempt for the town and its people for enabling such vile acts to transpire. A murderous rage had taken hold of Edmund, inflicting upon him an irreconcilable conscience retaliative to the loss of innocence.

"And what of the seventh soul? Who, pray tell, shall be the last to retribute the soul of Annie Mae?"

"The honor shall be yours, Resurrector; he who profits from the dead shall live among them."

"...So sayest thou, Spirit. Thy will shall be done..."

"Spare no moment, necromancer. The midnight hour fast approaches and I await my prize."

For the last time, the apparition vanished, never to be seen again. With nothing else to lose, Edmund took off toward the chapel to fulfill the devil's work and bring an end to his ill-spent life. It was the last that anyone would ever see of poor Edmund Raye.

***

The next day, a quiet morning dawned as the town awoke to a grizzly scene of murder and mutilation across Barrington. In the home of Mayor Caulfield, a housemaid discovered George and Cynthia in their bedroom asphyxiated, hanging from the chandelier. Despite every rationalization, no one could determine how they managed to reach the lighting fixture to hang themselves.

Near the center of town, the fetor of decay emanated from Dr. Penn's medical institute, leading the town to uncover many dark secrets remaining within. The bodies of Dr. Penn's handlers, Malcolm and Vincent, were found sitting upright in the pews of the auditorium, each missing their eyes, ears, and tongue. Inside Dr. Penn's chambers, Dr. Penn's remains were found among a scene of ritualistic sacrifice. His corpse, drenched in an unknown substance and displaying advanced stages of decayed flesh, lay under the guise of his fallen idol the demon Wendigo. Infected and highly contagious, Dr. Penn's remains became the source of a renewed outbreak of cholera throughout the land and had to be burned.

    Not far from Dr. Penn's medical institute, Father Campbell turned up dead inside Lord Haven's Parish. His body had been impaled onto the altar by a sharpened crucifix. Whoever had committed such a heinous act must have been a person of great strength, for no one could determine how the killer was capable of forcing such a large crucifix into the chest of Father Campbell. It was a horrific sight many found to be unwarranted until they discovered the remnants of Father Campbell's personal effects. In the parishioner's office, there existed a secret room behind a cabinet. The cabinet had been moved and the door to the secret room left ajar. Inside the room, the townsfolk uncovered a dungeon filled with torture devices and skeletons of dead children chained to the wall. Most of them were still in the process of decomposition. Every one of them, boy and girl, met a painful end at the hands of the priest.

But what remained a mystery at the time to the townsfolk that day was the whereabouts of Edmund Raye. His absence led many to believe that he was the murderer, but without any evidence, no one could be certain. It wasn't until a few days later that the townsfolk discovered the tombstone of Annie Mae Caulfield had been torn from the ground. The remaining members of the town dug up the coffin to ensure no one had tampered with Annie Mae's body. What they found in the coffin left everyone who was present speechless and horrified. Annie Mae was nowhere to be found! Instead, they discovered the body of Edmund Raye, buried alive as it were. On the lid of the coffin was a message that looked to have been carved by Edmund with nothing but his fingernails. The message read, "I shall be vindicated!"

Not long after the discovery of Edmund Raye and the gruesome Barrington murders, the townspeople had finally succumbed to disease, leaving the town dangerously few. After the Civil War, the town was completely abandoned. To this day, all that remains of Barrington are the overgrown ruins within the ancient Appalachian Forest. Rumors abound that few travelers who have passed close by the lands that were once Barrington can still hear the voices of the damned – chanting, cursing one another in eternal torment – and a woman clad in white seen wandering through the woods. The body of Annie Mae Caulfield was never found.

GROWING PAINS
Tyler Markham

Leslie stood in the warm spring rain and looked out at his field. A weed-filled hellscape with dirty water pooling in the low spots of the soil stared back at him, and he spat a mouthful of tobacco onto the dirt road. Damn corn seed never caught. Soil was all used up, he assumed, as he let the rain wet the sunburnt part of his neck.

His brow furrowed when his eyes scanned to his neighbor Thomas's plot, right next to his, green as he'd ever seen corn. The stalks stood hearty against the wind and the rain, and even though it was only the second week of June it was as high as his shoulders. How come his corn is looking so damn good? Just one foot off to the side is Leslie's own plot, and it was a stark contrast. His stomach grumbled and he left his tractor to walk back to the house. Every few moments he turned and stared confused at Thomas's field.

He stepped up his porch and took a seat next to his wife, Anne, who was busy fixing the stand mixer. Parts were littered all around, and she was twisting off the base with a screwdriver, her hair pinned back in a frizzy knot of gray curls.

"Not good, huh?" she said.

"You seen Thomas's plot?"

"What's a matter with it?"

"It's growing," he said.

She set down the little screwdriver she was using. "Is it now? How well?"

"Best corn I ever saw, I think."

She nodded and tried to crane her neck around the big tree at the bottom of the property, blocking Thomas's land. "Wonder what he's done."

"Same here."

"Couldn't you go ask him?"

Leslie laughed and kissed his wife on the forehead. "It'd take a lot more than what we've got going on to ask

Thomas for help. All the sum' bitch would do is wave it in my face."

Anne sighed, picked up her screwdriver again, and wrenched at the bolt. It needed some grease, or some elbow-grease, so Leslie tried to take the screwdriver from her and she snatched it away and held it close to her bosom.

"What is it?"

"Nothin'," she said. "I would get up and make you a sandwich but I'm busy here. Barely anything left in the fridge."

Leslie tried his best not to slam the screen door on his way in. Did she expect him to get on his knees and beg for Thomas's help? A man doesn't beg for help. He works it out on his own. Especially if the man in question wouldn't lift a finger for anyone else but himself, his own wife included.

He grabbed two slices of bread and set them on his plate. He reached into the fridge without looking and came up with the bag of ham from the deli. There was barely enough for half a sandwich, but he made one anyway and sat at the table looking out at his field, eating in silence and thinking about the feed bill and the fertilizer bill and the electricity bill on the counter to his right like a burning pile of hay.

The next day Leslie was walking along the back of the house where the cow was fenced in with an empty pail of water. The well was dry. His face and hands were, too, and his underarms were beginning to sour.

He stepped into the house and Anne was sitting at the dinner table with a mess of flour and dough surrounding her. She still hadn't said a word to him.

"Wells dry," he said.

She kept kneading without even looking up. She looked like an angry thunder cloud to Leslie, white dust puffing around her as she worked.

He set the metal bucket onto the hardwood with a clatter and threw his hands in the air. "When are you going to stop ignoring me, huh? I ain't going to ask that, that… asshole, for any help. We been doing just fine on our own!"

Still, she stared at her work. Just kneading, back and forth with the force of an ox. When she got this way there was no telling when she'd snap out. Leslie was usually the first to cave, and he could feel his patience slipping already.

Leslie stepped around the table, took Anne's shoulders in his hands and stooped down to kiss her on the top of her head.

"If I go ask him, will ya talk to me?"

She stopped kneading, turned around with a smile and gave him a floury peck on his cheek that he savored before wiping it off.

"You ol' ball buster," he said, laughing as he left out of the door towards his truck.

As he drove down the winding dirt drive that led to the main road, Leslie hoped Thomas wasn't home so he could come back and say he tried. They had to do something about the crops, he knew that, but did it have to come from Thomas?

When he pulled up at the end of his dirt drive he tried to make sense of the way the corn was growing. Was it water? New seed? Fertilizer Leslie had never heard of? It seemed to grow an inch taller just to spite him.

Thomas must've heard his truck. He was coming out of his barn with the biggest grin Leslie had ever seen. It took everything out of him not to turn around and hang up his hat for good. Screw the farm, he could find something else to do with his land. Raise cows or horses, he thought, but no one would bankroll that. Especially for a sixty-year-old man and his wife.

"Leslie, my boy," Thomas yelled. Leslie hated it when he called him that. The man was ten years his junior.

"Corn's doing decent this year, ain't it."

Thomas's smile widened, showing a missing tooth Leslie never noticed. "I'd say so for myself, but by the looks of your plot you haven't had the same luck."

Leslie stepped down out of his truck with a groan. "Boy, we both know you ain't good enough of a farmer to pull something like this off."

"Looks like I am," he said.

Leslie looked back towards the hill where his house sat, saw the big tree he had planted with his grandpa as a kid, could smell the dusty barn. Could see in his mind's eye Anne sitting on the porch tinkering away at something. He swallowed hard and hung his head. "I don't think you understand how much this pains me, Thomas," he said. For some reason, he felt like crying. "Me and Anne aren't doing so hot right now–"

"We're no charity organization over here, you–"

"Would you shut your damn mouth and let me talk?" Leslie said. "What did you do to get this corn to grow? D'you get irrigation installed? If so, I don't know how you bankrolled it."

"Nope," he said.

"Fertilizer or something?"

Thomas shook his head. "Just this old green thumb of mine, Leslie, if you want some lessons I'd be happy to give them to you."

Without another word, Leslie turned and stepped back up onto his truck.

"Wait, Leslie. I'm sorry. I'm sorry." he said. "I'm just pulling your leg. I've been meaning to tell someone. It's been eating me up a bit, to be honest with you."

"What is?"

"How I got this corn here to grow."

Thomas walked Leslie across his yard and into his barn. All the tools that a man needs were gone. No tractor in the barn, no feeder or fertilizer.

"Where's all your shit, Thomas? Up and sell it?"

"Had to pay the bills somehow," he said. "Here, come look at this." Leslie noticed that Thomas was shaking, from excitement or anxiety, he wasn't sure, but the kid was giving him the creeps with how worked up he was. There was a tarp at the end of the long barn covering a small corner of his work bench. Thomas pulled the cover-up just enough for him to grab something out of it. It was a small glass bottle. Inside it was something Leslie had never seen before. It was a red-tainted liquid, like a strawberry jam of sorts, except thinner.

"The hell's that?"

Thomas set it on the table and addressed Leslie. The shaking had stopped. "You can't tell a soul Leslie. Not one person, you hear me? I've been keeping this a secret for so long now I don't know how it hasn't ate me all the way up. I was nearly bursting with the guilt of it."

"Get on with it, now," Leslie said.

"You ever heard of blood meal?"

Leslie laughed. "Boy, tell me you ain't sell everything you got for some blood meal? Is that it?"

Thomas's face soured and he grabbed the little bottle like a kid. Leslie almost laughed at the absurdity of it, but thought wiser when he saw the image of his wife scowling in bed next to him.

"It's not blood meal you old coot. Similar, I guess, but no. It's my own."

"Your own what?"

"My blood."

Leslie took a step back. "You gone nuts in the heat."

"Don't you get all spooked, now. You came here asking me for help and I'm doing you a damn favor. Could've kept this to myself."

"Could you? Looks like you was damn near bursting at the seams to tell someone."

Thomas's face got red. "Screw you then, you and yours can starve."

"No, no. I want to hear it. Go on now. I hate to say it but I'd do about anything now."

Thomas grabbed the jar back up and nodded for Leslie to follow him. They walked out of the back of the barn and down the fifty-foot dirt lane to the start of his field. Thomas uncorked the bottle and waited for Leslie to catch up.

"I read some time ago that Native Americans used to use their blood for farming. Something about giving yourself to the land and all that. They'd mix their blood with bunches of berries or something and water and pour it onto the land they planned on planting, and it helped." Thomas rubbed the back of his sunburnt neck and looked out over the cornfield. "Do you believe in God, Leslie?"

"Course I do, but the way you're talking I don't think you're talking about God, son. You sure you ain't gotten too much sun lately? You're talking gibberish."

"I ain't talkin gibberish," Thomas said. He capped the bottle again and regarded Leslie with a sun-blistered scowl. "I was doing something nice for you, ya know, trying to help out and this is what you do to me? Screw you, then, I don't need you."

Thomas walked off. Leslie wasn't going to stop him. The sumbitch wasn't sharing his secret. So be it. He never wanted his darn help anyway.

He walked across Thomas's lawn and hopped back into his truck. As he drove by the corn, then past his dirt patch, he thought of the little red bottle.

"Well, what'd he say?" Anne asked. She was sitting on the porch letting the sun bathe her. She looked skinnier. Less solid than when he met her at eighteen, poor and dirty at her own pa's farm.

"I think he's gone mad," he said. "We got any tea?"

"Out."

Leslie sighed. "Anything we ain't out of?"

"Air and dirt."

Leslie took a seat next to his wife in the little rocking chair and looked out. Down the hill, the grass was green in little tufts, and the rest was covered by dust. "You wanna know what he said?"

"I asked you, didn't I?" she said.

"God damn sol' off all his stuff. He's fertilizing the plants with his blood."

Anne shot up out of her chair. "He said what?"

"What? He been using his blood. I told you he was acting crazy. Thought he may have found some damn new seeds or something or other, but I guess he doesn't want to tell us old folks. Probably trying to buy our land or something."

Anne took one of Leslie's hands in hers, her deep wrinkles tickling his dry hands, and placed another on his face to turn him towards her.

The last time she saw her this serious she was picking him up drunker than a skunk from Dan's Place up town.

"I want you to listen to me, you hear? Don't you listen to him. That ain't nothin to mess with"

"Why the hell would I do something like that?"

Anne squeezed his hand. "Because you're a good man trying to feed his family. We'll make do, and you don't need to be doing any of that. Do you hear me?"

"Yes ma'am," he said. She let go. They both looked off down the hill at their empty field.

Leslie was coming back from the barn with feed the next day when the tractor started to smoke.

"Shit," he whispered to himself. He jumped down and lifted the hood to check what may be going on, and noticed that one of the piston rings was broken. He'd have to walk all the way back to the barn to look for one when he was ninety percent sure he didn't have one. If he didn't, he'd have to go into town to the tractor supply and by the time he got back his old bones may be too tired to handle the change.

He sat on the foot of the tractor and looked out over his yard, and down the hill towards Thomas's. Never in any world would he have thought to ask Thomas for help, but since the last day he had thought of him more and more.

Corn doesn't just grow like that. Shit, it almost seemed a foot taller now as he looked at it.

Maybe Thomas would have a piston ring.

When he got to Thomas's, one of the cars was missing. He knocked on the barn door and peeked his head in. "Thomas?" he said, but the echo let him know that no one was there. Fine enough. He'd get him when he came back. But what if they're gone long? He's got work to get to, the little work he has. His mind went back to the little red bottle again, and the thought occurred to him. What would it hurt? Shit, Thomas was messing with him, he was almost certain about that, but on the off chance that this hokie shit worked, why not give it a try? Anne had warned him against it but what did she know about Native Americans? Not more than him, that's for sure.

He walked down the dirt road and looked at the stark difference between the fields. The waving, green, healthy corn on Thomas's plot, and his dirt patch with raggedy stalks a brief break of wind might knock over.

He found himself in the barn without much recollection of how he got there. He had a bottle in his hand, and a little kitchen knife in the other. Little slits of sunlight were coming in between the slats creating a prison of light beams surrounding Leslie. He hesitated as he brought the blade up to the back of his skin, then laughed to himself. Most of their savings were gone, and instead of doing something, he was following Thomas. What had the world come to? His world, at least, had come to a halt.

He dug the knife into the back of his liver-spotted hand. The skin shifted and moved under it like the bladder of a gutted mule until a little red patch showed. It trickled down his hand and onto the dirt floor of the barn, turning dark as it sucked the dirt up until it was unnoticeable.

He checked over his shoulder, just to be sure Anne wasn't there, and let a couple of crimson drops muddy the waters until it looked like syrup. He swished it around and held it up to his face.

"My body to the land," he said with a shake of his head and a laugh, and walked out of the barn and into the field.

He didn't know how much he should use, if this little bit was going to do anything, hell, it wasn't, but at this point what else was there to do? He had used up the rest of the money for the best fertilizer, the best corn seed he could buy, but the land was all used up.

He tipped the bottle into the dirt and watched the land suck it up like a greedy child at his mother's teat. The scorched dirt muddied for a brief moment before slowly returning to its dry alligator skin. He felt like a fool. An old fool who'd run out of luck after all these years. He laughed to himself, shook his head, and stuffed the little empty bottle into his back pocket. He decided he wouldn't mention it to Anne. They'd had enough fighting lately.

After all the walking he did that day, the porch looked wonderfully comfortable, so he sat on it and began rocking. He didn't even know he had fallen asleep until he was shaken awake by Anne.

It was storming, wind howling against the house, throwing the final wisps of his hair back on his head.

"What's a matter?" he said. Anne's face was full of wonder, her eyes sparkling and ageless. Could have been a childs if it wasn't for the wrinkles at their corners.

"Hun, the corn. The corn!"

He sprang up, tweaking something in his back. But it didn't matter. The once barren, weed-littered plot of land was showing signs of growth. Not entirely, but right in the middle where he had spilled the bottle, corn was sprouting.

"Good thing we got that fertilizer this year, thought we was gonna be a goner," she said. Leslie couldn't find the words. It was probably the rain, after all, but the coincidence was just too grand to ignore.

Anne clasped her hands together and looked around for something to do. "Know what I'm gonna do tonight? Gonna cook us up a good supper. Cornbread. Maybe some potatoes. What do you think about a chicken fried steak?"

His eyes were still on the corn. "Sure, hun, yeah, that sounds wonderful."

"I gotta get to the store, " she said. "Need anything?"

"Bottle of bourbon if we can muster it."

Anne cooked one of the best-looking dinners Leslie had ever seen. The cornbread was moist, smothered in honey butter. The potatoes were just how he liked them, smothered in butter, too, and doused in salt. The steak was fried to perfection, with little crispy edges on it. He could barely stomach it.

"Maybe we can finally repaint the barn," Anne said. Leslie felt something in the pit of his stomach. He wasn't sure whether it was guilt or excitement, but he felt wrong about the whole thing. Like he had cheated. Sometimes, though, he tried to convince himself it was alright. They were always good people. Helped out their neighbors, raised good kids, and always went to church on Sundays. It was their turn to be lucky.

"Maybe we can," he said. "Gotta get this corn grown first."

He helped Anne clean up dinner, and as he dried the cast iron, he couldn't help but take in the sight of the corn. He didn't know if it was a trick of the fading sun but it sprouted more, god darn it. He thought of the bourbon. Whether he liked Thomas or not, that was beside the point. Maybe he'd go over there and share a swig with him, even if the damn blood hadn't helped. It didn't of course, but that was the neighborly thing to do, after all.

"Hun, mind finishin' up here? Thinking of goin over to Thomas's. Share a little of this whiskey with him."

She stopped washing, her sleeves wet up to her elbow. "Why in the heck would you do that?"

"Well–" and he couldn't think of an excuse.

"Leslie," she said. "You didn't do what he tol' you to, did ya?"

"What? With the blood? Course not, why would I do such a silly thing like that?"

Her eyes searched his face for a sign of a lie, whether she decided to forget it or not, or disregard the bandage on the back of his hand, he wasn't sure, but she smiled. "Alright, go on now. I'll be on the porch when you get back."

He grabbed the bottle and walked down the hill to Thomas's.

Their car was back, the lights flickering in their windows. He knocked on the door and waited, and Thomas's wife, Carla, opened up. His smile dropped immediately. Her hair looked white as a sheet.

"What's going on, Carla? Everything alright?"

She shook her head, tears fighting against her lower lids. "Thomas's sick."

"Oh, I was gonna share this bottle a bit with him. Mind if I go have a word with him? He decent?"

She nodded and stepped out of the way. "Two doors down the hall," she said.

His legs were far away under him as he walked. He opened the door and there Thomas was, sitting upright, and holding his gut.

"What happened to you?"

"Close that damn door, Leslie." He did and set the bottle on the dresser to the right. Thomas was groaning. "You close that door tight?"

"What happened to you?"

Thomas was sweating. "You didn't do what I told you, did ya?"

"Well, yeah, I did, but I'm sure it was nothing."

He let out a groan again. "My kidneys gone," he said.

Leslie's mouth opened and closed. "I didn't know you was sick."

"I ain't sick," he said. "They didn't remove it. It's gone. Disappeared. Same with these."

His hands made their way up to his mouth. He pulled the lips up, and the one tooth that he noticed was missing the other day was accompanied by ten more.

"Jesus Christ," Leslie said. He ran his tongue over his teeth. They were in there, as solid as they could be at his age.

"I'm sorry Leslie, I–" he coughed, shaking his entire frame. There was a rag next to him that he spat in, and it was red, just like the little red bottle. "I shouldn't a told ya. I'm sorry. I was just trying to help, ya know, feed my family. Shouldn't a done it."

Leslie was sitting there trying to listen but he kept tonguing his teeth, trying to find the hiding, rotting tooth but it wasn't there.

"Is there any way you can stop it?" Leslie asked.

Thomas shrugged. "Don't know, but I think it's too late for me, after all. Again, I'm sorry Leslie."

Leslie stood and walked out without another word. He left the bottle.

When he got home Anne was sitting on the porch. She was sipping on a cup of coffee, and he walked right past her, up the stairs, and laid in bed staring at the ceiling.

Thomas was dead the next day. The only reason they found out was because Anne had seen the hearse pull past their house to Thomas's. Leslie tried to figure out everything he could from Anne, but all she said was. "Found him keeled over next to his plot with a thing of gasoline. Don't know what happened to him, but that's what Carla said over the phone."

Leslie sat at breakfast and took a bite of his eggs when he felt an emptiness in his mouth. He felt with his tongue, then his finger. A molar was gone. Anne was sitting across from him humming, working on some crochet she hadn't touched in months. He didn't know if he'd ever seen her so happy, finally relieved that their troubles were over. His stomach turned, and his mind went to Thomas, out at night by the corn, ready to light it all up. What had busted or disappeared? His heart? His brain? A lung? He didn't know.

He stood. "I'll be back in a minute," he said. Anne smiled and kept knotting away. He needed to see something.

He was standing in front of Thomas's corn now. The closer he got to it, he started to notice there was something off. Sure, it was green, standing tall in the wind, but it was too tall for this time of year. It didn't sway right. When the wind went left some went right or stayed still. It was as if they were moving on their own, each stalk a sentient being. He crept closer, and all at once the stalks seemed to freeze as if seen by a predator. It wasn't right. None of it was. When he got close enough to see the little hairs coming from the top of the corn, he saw something was oozing from one of them. A red substance of sorts, dripping from a leaf and into the soil, just like the little vial of red Leslie had emptied into his own plot the day prior. He approached one of them with his knife in hand, as if the things would come alive, and cut a small ear off of it. He peeled, yelled out, and dropped the damn thing. There may have been a husk, but what was inside made Leslie throw up in the soil.

The corn, or whatever the hell it was, did not grow. It was replaced by a red, oozing mass, and stuck into this mass everywhere like kernels were molars. Molars of different sizes, colors of actual corn or the dark gray color of rot and decay. His eyes were blurred by tears and all around him it felt like the field was willing pain on his heart. He inhaled shakily, stared at his own plot and felt in his mouth with his tongue, where the tooth was missing. He thought of Thomas standing outside of his plot in his underwear with a box of matches and a can of gasoline.

He knew what he had to do.

He was dousing the small circle of corn in the center of his plot with gasoline when Anne ran up behind him. "What the hell do you think you're doing?"

All he had to do was give her a look, and she knew. She knew that he'd done what he had to, but still, it made her face twist into a mask of despair. He stepped far enough away from the field and struck a match. Anne was beating on his arms, begging him to stop, but he threw it anyway. The second the match hit the dirt and ignited, crawling to the corn and its brothers, Leslie felt his skin getting hot, slowly, at first, like a sunburn. Before he could draw another breath it became a searing pain equivalent to nothing he'd felt before. He wiped at himself, looked down for a fire but saw nothing. It started at his feet, then his legs, crawling up to his chest.

"Oh, lord Jesus!" he screamed. It was as if the fire had crawled up into his skin and laid dormant there. Begging to get out from him. He dropped to his knees and the world narrowed to a pinhole, the agony forcing his eyes shut. His beautiful wife's face was the last thing he saw before an invisible fire ravaged not his outer body, his skin or hair, but his innards. His heart became a molten mass, and from his ear a single drop of blood leaked into the soil and disappeared.

Anne buried her husband a week later. She came home and sat on the porch. Out in the field, the corn was growing again, but this time, it came in slow and steady. Natural. She wept into her hands. The can of gasoline sat next to her full, with a box of matches ready at her side.

THE BRIDES
Michael Bertolini

Tomas James had always had a fascination with flowers. His father was a florist in the nearby village and had taught Tomas so much of what he knew, to the point that Tomas was given the honor of arranging the flowers for his father's funeral. Thirty years after he began learning the craft, now at the age of 39, Tomas was in heaven. To say that it was easy would be a lie, he'd often find that he needed to clean up after the wolves that ran through the garden or dispose of the cloth bags that were occasionally there as though victims of the same horrific wind that threatened to break his precious flowers. He never questioned the presence of wolf tracks, even though he was well aware that the entire garden was surrounded by iron fences and stone walls, nor did he ever wonder why the bags always appeared somewhat shredded by animal claws and stained by an ichor that resembled drying blood.

The sky was turning dark as Tomas finished pruning, the moon his only light before frost threatened to coat his beloved flowers and kill whatever wasn't ready to survive the cold. The butler, Edgar, had warned Tomas to stay away from the castle at night, and the master of the castle had issued a similar warning, but Tomas was unaware of the deepening purple of the sky as he stood from where he knelt among the roses and made his way to the gate that marked the garden's exit. It was a winding path and any unaware visitor might easily be confused about the correct path to take, but Tomas had no fear of confusion.

Standing between him and the gate was a young woman, likely in her mid to upper twenties, standing on the gravel path and smelling a flower. She seemed oblivious to Tomas' appearance and he didn't know what to make of her, Edgar had never made any allusion to a woman on the property, especially one as young and bewitching as the woman in the garden, but he was sure that the topic slipped his elderly mind as so many things were common to do.

"I've always wanted to meet the man who took care of these beautiful flowers." She spoke in a soft, almost whimsical voice. She was thin with sharp angles of her face and pale skin. Her blonde hair draped down in thin waves to her silk robe which left little to the imagination as it conformed to the curves of her body. Tomas felt himself swell but remembered the vow he made to his wife before God and cleared his throat. She smiled.

"I'm glad that you enjoy them."

"My sister has no consideration of such beauty." He realized that, while she spoke Romanian, her accent was foreign and he tried to place it. For some reason, he thought that the man in the village, the rabbi from Israel, could help. She turned and Tomas could see her beauty; she had crystal blue eyes and thin, red lips. Her robe slipped open a little and he could easily see that she wore nothing under it despite the chill tickling the night air; the curves of her breasts lured his eyes and the shadows concealing her made him momentarily forget about his wife Florina. Her hips were curved though she wasn't wide; in fact, she almost appeared frail and emaciated despite her obvious imperviousness to the growing cold. "My name is Michaela."

"Tomas."

"I know. My husband hired you to tend his garden since Edgar has so many other duties around the castle," she gave a soft laugh, "and I think Edgar is too old to consider such beauty."

"Your husband?" Tomas immediately adverted his eyes bowed slightly. "I apologize if I offended you." He blushed but noticed that she did not; he realized that her skin never changed color or gave any indication of reaction to the cold. He reasoned that the flowers must be chilled and a quick touch would've proven him correct if he was able to move from her sight.

"Not at all." She smiled as she walked forward, the robe billowing open to reveal her entire body: her flawless ivory skin and long, seductive legs. "In truth, he has little time for me with his business dealings around the world. You, on the other hand, have no such qualms. You look at my body and I can feel the lust like flames licking my skin." She put one hand on his right arm and the other slid into his pants. "Your secret desire is growing in my hand."

Tomas' eyes started to close as she stroked, his head lolling to the side as the faint outline of the master of the house seemed to materialize out of the shadows. But the man didn't move, he just stood and watched as his bride seduced another man. Even as Michaela leaned closer and began to kiss Tomas' neck, he didn't move. He could sense her lips gingerly caressing his skin while her tongue traced the outlines created by the veins and muscles and sinew of his throat. She leaned close and he could feel her breasts, also unaffected by the cold, pressed into him. He wanted her, he damned Florina and silently vowed that he would take Michaela.

He didn't register the bite immediately. Her canines, long and thin, pierced his neck like a thirsting mosquito. He was immediately overcome by a wave of delirium as if his mind was under the influence of one of the many hallucinogen poisons the garden concocted as a defense against preying insects. His mind became a hallucinogenic dream as Michaela drank from him, his life draining. He half remembered the mention of a curse on the castle and its inhabitants, a tale he'd chalked up to fear and distrust. Tomas knew the truth and soon lost the ability to stand as there was not enough blood flowing into his limbs. Michaela had no trouble forcing him to the ground where his spine broke under the pressure of her animalistic strength.

Many would say that she drank too much, that she drank until her thirst was sated and Tomas' life was at an end, but Michaela would disagree. Her sister and she were given paltry meals of infants stolen from their cribs. Their master wouldn't let them touch Edgar or his English guest. As to be expected, Michaela's sister was there but she was too late to enjoy the rich blood that filled Michaela's stomach. Once they were convened, their master approached with his gaze on Tomas' corpse.

"Poor Tomas," he said with a thick accent, "I warned you to leave before dark and now, unfortunately, you leave me no choice." His eyes violently jerked up toward the two women standing before him and he brushed a loose strand of hair away from his eyes. "Tomas had a wife and child in the village, they will seek justice. Be sure that they are removed."

One of the sisters, the brunette, Monica, stepped forward. "Are we able to feed?"

"Make sure that they don't become one of us," the master said, "and Michaela has already fed on poor Tomas."

He knelt beside the now cold corpse of Tomas and plunged his sharp fingers into the unfortunate gardener's chest to tear out his heart. He discarded the still-beating organ to the white and red flowers and proceeded to separate the head from the body. "I am sorry, but you leave me no choice." He made sure to toss the head a few yards away before standing. He spoke to the sisters as he brushed any disturbing remaining dirt off of his clothes, it wouldn't do good if his guest were to see. "Be off and remember to return before sunrise."

    The women chuckled as their bodies and thin robes exploded into thousands of bugs that immediately started to fly away. Each bug resembled a fly, the cloud of flies that had been Monica swept over the corpse abandoned by Tomas and consumed all of the flesh it could, each swelling in size just a little as all they left were bones. Rising into the sky, high above the winding trail that a carriage would've been forced to take, the flies descended upon the village like a plague ready to be unleashed.

    Florina James stood at the window of the cottage owned by her husband, the infant girl in the back room already sleeping, waiting for a sign of Tomas' return. He knew that the journey down the road from the castle was long, it wound to avoid taking a sharp plunge but that meant a journey could easily take a few hours. But it was late, the moon was in the sky, and Tomas should've been home. Florina was not overly given to troubled thoughts but the idea of being employed by such a cursed creature as the master of the castle sent shivers down her spine. The rumors ran rampant that a former owner of the castle, a few generations past, had been a fierce warrior who spilled the blood of so many innocents that the very stones of the castle were forever stained in the blood of his victims and they, ghosts lost and unable to go to God, cursed the land.

The ravine that separated the village from the castle was the only barrier to hold back the poison yet Tomas had always been adamant that the ground around the castle was fertile and lively.

A stiff breeze blew some of the trees that stood near the cottage and a knock came to the door which confused Florina; she'd been watching out the window and was in a position to see an approach. She hesitated for a moment before resolving herself with her head held high against the dark rising around the cottage.

"Hello?" She called, her heavy Romanian accent strong with no indication of the fear she truly felt. A delay could've meant many things but this strange knock from an unseen visitor only compounded the possible horror that had washed from the castle like a wave of terror.

"Florina?" A weak, female voice uttered in confusion as though the owner wasn't sure that she was even at the right door.

"Yes?"

"Oh, I've the right house!" The voice seemed almost cheerful at the notion. "Tomas sent me to send you a message, he'd been injured and a doctor is up at the castle to treat him, but I doubt that he'll be home any time soon." Florina sighed, her ears missing the soft chuckle from the two voices on the opposite side of the door. "Might I come in?"

"Oh, please, of course." Tomas had mentioned other staff at the castle but hadn't been clear on any of their identities, so she had no reason to think that there was any malicious intent.

"Your invitation is appreciated." The voice, much more powerful than the mousey nature it possessed before, boomed as the door burst open. Thousands of flies buzzed in with enough force to strike Florina in the chest and push her back. Florina sat on the floor, coughing, as the flies coalesced into two young women, a blonde and a brunette equally thin and equally pale. "It's nice to finally meet you. I'm Michaela and this is Monica." The blonde woman who had given the weak voice at the door chuckled.

The brunette knelt, her visible body producing crescent shadows that would make many of the men in the village cry in desperation and disappointment. The baby in the back room started to cry when Michaela spoke. Monica turned to Michaela and jerked her head. "Take care of it."

"My pleasure."

"But don't kill it," Monica said, "we might want the snack." Michaela shrugged and walked through the closed door to the dark room beyond. The baby's cries intensified and Florina's eyes went wide when she heard the thump of something soft hitting a wooden surface with enough force to expel all of life from it. The thump repeated two more times. Florina screamed in horror as Michaela reappeared with gore-covered hands.

"Sorry."

"It's fine," Monica shrugged as she turned back to Florina. "We've already eaten, the snack is unnecessary." Florina gasped as she heard the words that confirmed her fear, that Tomas had been a meal for a monster and wouldn't be running through the door to save the day; and, as it sounded, the women were the monsters. She knew who was responsible for killing her child, that much was clear, but she didn't know the brunette's role in all of this.

Monica pushed Florina's head back forcefully, bit into her jugular, and swallowed the sweet, thick nectar of blood that flowed into her mouth. Her eyes closed in relaxed euphoria.

She was surprised when Florina pushed her back. Monica hissed, no human had ever before been able to resist the mesmerizing narcotic effect of the bite. She was about to lunge forward again, to resume drinking even if it meant breaking Florina's bones into compliance when the woman grabbed a candle and drove the burning flame into her left eye. Monica screamed. Vampires only had a few weaknesses, the main one affecting most, but not all, being direct sunlight which could burn their exposed flesh. They all were, however, susceptible to a few more things that humanity had learned over the years; including fire. While unable to match the intensity of sunlight, fire consumed them like dry leaves. They withered, they burned uncontrollably, they were destroyed.

Monica reeled back, the fire was too small to consume her entirely but not too insignificant to leave a lasting impression, and Michaela stepped forward.

"What did you do?"

"Get out of my house, you aren't welcome in this place of God." Michaela followed Florina's gaze to the crucifix hanging on the wall as part of a small shrine that Tomas had built. Florna smiled, thinking that she'd won, but Michael shook her head.

"It doesn't work that way," Michaela said, "all of your stories about running water, garlic, and invitation aren't real. They're just in place to make you comfortable, to make you calm, that you have power over the monsters that stalk you."

"Will a stake to the heart end your poor existence?"

"I don't know," Michaela spread her robe to clearly show the path through her chest and her bare breasts, she wondered at the possibility of straining Florina's lust enough to use it against her, "do you want to stick me? I've never been... impaled... like that." She took Florina's hand, gingerly getting her to release the candle holder clenched in her fingers, and used Florina's thin fingers to touch the area of her chest nearest her heart which happened to coincide with her fingers gingerly tracing the curves of her breasts.

"You came here to kill me," Florina spoke in such a sultry way that it took Michaela a moment to understand the words, "you should've done it." Before she could react, Florina shoved Michaela backward and ran for the open door. She half noted that Monica was starting to rise as she skipped past. Florina wanted to go to her baby, to see if it was alright, but Michaela had discarded the poor infant like a piece of trash and Florina was confident that she no longer lived.

Florina only managed to run fifty yards before Michaela and Monica caught up to her. She was out of breath, pain wracked her lungs as the acid inside burned, and she had to put her hands on her knees to keep from falling as she took deep gasps of air. Michaela and Monica didn't seem perturbed at all.

"Please." Florina gasped.

"She begs?" Monica looked at Michaela.

"Please what? Please stay away. Please let me live. Please let it be quick!" Michaela started to laugh.

"Please," Florina said as she felt the small blade, the kitchen utensil she'd grabbed in her mad dash, slide from its hiding place, "come closer." She turned and stabbed Michaela in the chest but missed her heart. The injury still hurt and the vampire slunk away as Monica grabbed Florina's arm and snapped it back until the bones broke in protest. Monica kicked Florina's legs out, forcing her to her knees.

"Your death will be slow." Monica bit down on Florina's neck and began to feed. Florina's arms went limp and her body spasmed with every gulp. After several tense seconds, Florina took her final breath and her heart stopped. Monica dropped the cold corpse to the dirt and looked at Michaela. Her sister, not really her sister, young and blonde with vigor and foolishness, was barely maintaining her consciousness. The blade had missed its target but Michaela would be slow until her body healed; had she not feared the master's wrath, she'd leave Michaela to suffer the consequences of her own making. But, rather than that,

Monica helped Michaela stand and the two walked together up the mountain, stealing horses when it was appropriate.

It was nearing dawn when Monica and Michaela returned to the castle. Edgar was outside, already prepared to put the horses in the stall while the master stood at the threshold, arms folded. The two women stopped, Michaela, holding a hand over her chest where the knife had punctured. The master looked at both and sneered while Edgar moved away from the women toward the single closed castle door.

"Secrecy is our currency here and secrecy must be maintained," the master said in a deep, booming voice that was more akin to his stern speech than any other tone he'd ever used, "no stranger has ever come to my door since a Turk assassin with the same desire to end my existence, no stranger has known my true name. But you two let my secret out into the world," he took several steps forward, "and the secret came." He turned and nodded to Edgar who opened the closed castle door to reveal someone standing on the opposite side, a woman with long dark hair and simple clothing still stained by dirt, sweat, and blood.

"It's not possible," Monica said as her eyes went wide. "I took her life, I felt her die."

"The blood of a vampire is given in bite. If someone dies, drained of life, but consumes even a drop of a vampire's blood, that mortal may become one of us. You must remove the head to prevent the transformation. You know this, yet you didn't do it, and our secret is more than a fairytale." He turned and extended a hand to Florina who calmly walked out of the castle. "I instructed you *not* to make more of our kind and you disobeyed me! Dear Florina will have the honor of being my bride and forever your sister."

IN THE SHADOWS
Alan Dark

"There it is." Richie pointed to the clearing just above the road on a small hill. The dirt road curved just before the campsite and widened enough for them to park the jeep at the base of the hill. Richie smiled but nobody else in the car seemed to care; they agreed to go camping because Richie wanted to. Besides, as Richie promised Brian, there'd be plenty of opportunity to get alone time with the girls. Richie and Brian had been best friends since elementary school; Richie and Brian had gotten into a fistfight in the schoolyard and it was decided to give them both detention, together. They properly met, had a long whispered conversation that went unnoticed, and they were friends.

Now, in the last year of high school, both had girlfriends that, like all things in life, they shared. As far as the rest of the world was concerned, Richie was dating Stacy while Brian was dating Ashley; but Stacy's pregnancy scare came after she slept with Brian and Ashley had been with Richie more often than she'd been with Brian. Ashley wanted to exclusively date Richie but Stacy had beaten her to that.

"It looks a little," Brian frowned as he somehow managed to keep his composure and his voice steady, "dead." Brian was in the back seat with Ashley, his hand on her thigh and inching between her legs, Brian was a strong kid, everyone's favorite football star at school, and handsome enough for several girls to swoon in front of him; he cheated on Ashley often enough but he didn't think there was any reason to tell her about it. Ashley already had one hand on Brian's crotch stroking his dick through his pants, while her other hand had slipped into her own jeans; she was thinking about Richie while she played with herself, even though Brian was close enough to pleasure her.

"I think it looks fantastic, babe," Stacy smiled as she looked around, "though I think it's a little late in the season to be camping; I didn't see anyone else here."

"It'll be more private." Richie said.

"It's also cold."

"Don't worry, we can share a sleeping bag."

"Really?" She asked, biting her lower lip sensually, They set up camp quickly, the couples arranging their tents facing the fire and close enough should anyone want to slip into the other tent. When all was settled, they sat around the fire to each dinner and got drunk. Dinner consisted of hot dogs, which Stacy proceeded to lick seductively while looking at Brian. Everyone was getting drunk on the vodka Richie had brought to the point Ashley and Stacy were dancing around the fire, kissing each other as they passed in opposite circles. The girls stumbled on occasion, though it was clearly deliberate.

"Good night," Richie said to Brian as he and Stacy made their way to their tent and closed the zipper. From the sounds they loudly made, sleep was the last thing that they were doing. Brian chuckled as he heard Richie's heavy breathing get louder and louder; but he stopped paying attention when Ashley started rubbing her crotch.

"We should go into the tent." Brian said, his eyes fixated on Ashley.

"With them?" She asked playfully.

"No, our tent."

"If you insist," she pouted, "are you tired?"

"I will be once we're done." He smiled and she winked. As he stood, removing his shirt in a single flowing motion, Ashley followed. She undid each button of her sweater as she walked so that her top was off by the time Brian was closing the tent behind them.

Just before midnight, Brian groggily opened his eyes to the sounds of renewed sex in the other tent; he could almost imagine Stacy laying there while Richie loomed above her like a stalking predator, already deep inside of her. Ashley's dried juices were still on him but he didn't mind, she'd climaxed multiple times before he filled her.

"They should get some sleep." Brian mumbled before his eyes closed. Ashley, naked, smiled once Brian was asleep. She slipped out of the tent, naked, and into the other tent. She desperately wanted to join Richie and Stacy in their sleeping bag; she'd always fantasized about being with them both at the same time and, out in the wilderness with nobody around, it seemed to be a great time.

Richie didn't know which girl he'd finished in and, in his mind, it didn't matter. He watched them kiss and fondle each other in the moonlight that managed to shine through the roof of the tent. Growing up, visiting the campground with his family, he never imagined that he'd have his first three-some there; none of the other girls he'd been with wanted to share.

When he was done, and had collapsed onto his back, Ashley climbed on him and began grinding her hips. He knew that Stacy was crawling out of the sleeping bag, as naked as she was the day she was born, but he didn't care as Ashley stroked him erect and rode him.

They both froze when they heard Stacy scream.

They quickly grabbed shirts and rushed out of the tent while Brian ran out of his tent in the nude. What was left of Stacey was sprawled out on the ground near where the camo chairs had been set up near the fire. Her cherub face and angelic blonde hair had been ripped away and were nowhere to be seen while a large gash tore through her naked body from her navel to her throat. Her limbs still twitched nervously as the last of her life bled from her headless body, her organs aware that the end had arrived.

"What the hell is going on?" Brian yelled in terror. He rushed to Stacy and picked up her body, tears streaming down her face as she hung limp from his arms. Blood dripped down the curves of his muscles as her skin went cold to the touch and Brian gingerly laid her down, using a nearby blanket to cover her before he looked at his friend. "What did this?"

"I don't know," Richie stammered, "we were occupied." He held Ashley's hand.

"You brought us to this place," Brian stammered, "you must know something; are there bears in these woods?"

"No bears; but there were," Richie whispered, "stories. But they're just stories, who believes that crap aside from morons on the internet?" He shook his head while Ashley looked around.

"What are the stories?" She whimpered as she hugged herself, avoiding the rocks and twigs that threatened her bare feet.

"They're crazy," Richie growled, "stories say that some Native American shaman summoned some immortal beast to look after these lands. It's supposed to be taller than a man with thin arms, claws for teeth, antlers on its head, and hunger for human flesh." He laughed though he was unsure of things as he kept glancing around.

"Something clawed the shit out of her and took her head," Brian said as he stood, Stacy's viscera dripped down his torso, "monster or not, Stacy is dead."

"We should get out of here," Ashley whispered, "before it comes back." She started to walk toward the jeep, heedless that she was nearly naked, while Richie followed.

"Yeah, that's a good idea," Richie said with more confidence in his voice, "people in horror movies never get out when they have the chance." He said just before something heavy and quick tackled him to the ground in a blur of motion. Ashley backed away while Brian grabbed a branch they'd used for smores just a few hours earlier and brandished it as a weapon.

Something was quickly tearing at Richie's chest, his skin flaying and his ribs breaking. He managed to scream in terror just before a clawed hand grabbed him by the jaw and jerked back, tearing it away. Richie made a guttural plea for mercy but the creature didn't stop. He stopped moving, a look of serenity on his face. Before Brian could reach his friend, Richie was dead.

"Jesus fuck!" Brian exclaimed as the creature, the monster that had slaughtered Stacy and Richie, stood. It was well over seven feet tall and possessed long arms and legs tipped with claws. The creature was completely bald, its head adorned with twisting, unnatural antlers, and its eyes burned with a fury Brian had never seen before.

"What are you?" Brian yelled as he stepped back, now fully aware that he stood naked and defenseless against a monster that had no problem tearing flesh away. He glanced at Ashley and, as she slowly backed away, he decided. "Run Ashley, get out of here and get help," he turned his attention back to the monster, "come to me, you fucking piece of shit!"

The creature lept in his direction but sank into the ground as Brian moved in a vain attempt to get away from it. He turned, saw Ashley standing frozen, and yelled to her.

"Get out of here! Go!"

The creature pivoted in the dirt and lunged like a cat, sweeping its clawed hand across Brian's bare back. He keeled over as a line of red crossed his body, rolling with the momentum over rocks and broken tree limbs. A part of his mind went back to the days his mother would scold him for getting dirt in a fresh cut, warning him about infection; that, he mused, he wished would be the worst of his problems.

The creature dragged him to it and positioned itself above him, arms and legs splayed to hold Brian immobile. Brian, lying on his back, recognized the human features that the monster possessed; from the angles of its face to the spark of intelligence in its otherwise hate-filled eyes.

"You," Brian coughed blood as the monster squeezed his limbs, "aren't too smart if you fell for that distraction." He laughed and the monster leaned into Brian's face. Brian had to stop himself from smiling. The creature turned its head just as Ashley reached the jeep door and yanked it open. "You're too late, fucker."

Absently, the creature swung its arm like a pendulum, and the tip of a nail cut cleanly through Brian's neck. He wasn't dead so he felt every drop of blood leave his body. The creature turned back to Brian and smiled just before it tore Brian's penis away. Brian screamed in a combination of pain and horror. The creature tossed it away as blood poured from his crotch, though nowhere near as torrential as the blood pouring from Brian's throat. It bit down on Brian's ear and jerked its head, tearing the ear away, its prize able to easily slide into its gut. Brian yelled in pain but was able to muster a smile when he heard the Jeep's engine turn over.

"Ashley," Brian coughed, "got away." His heart stopped beating and the creature rose to its feet, Brian was already cold and it didn't like cold meat.

The creature let out a slow gasp of air, blood dripping from its bat-like maw, as the air began to ripple around it. It let out a simple dog-like bark and leaned back into the ripple; in an instant, it was gone and Brian was laying on his back.

Ashley drove furiously, it wasn't a long drive to the ranger station but the road was narrow and curved. She yelped in surprise when the air in front of the jeep rippled, almost like it was hot, and the monster landed on te hood of the jeep. This close, despite the pale moonlight, she was able to see it clearly; she could see the human features of its face staring at her with hate-filled eyes and the thin membrane that stretched along its arms like incomplete wings. It grabbed hold of the hood, swaying as Ashley tried her best to stay on the road. It opened its blood-stained mouth, revealing rows of small hooked teeth, and let out an ear-piercing shriek that made the glass between Ashley and it shatter. The creature reached forward, grabbed the steering wheel with a blood-soaked clawed hand, and jerked it to the side.

In her rush to get away, she hadn't bothered with the seatbelt so she was thrown.

Ashley skidded to a stop at the edge of the gravel parking area outside of the ranger station. She winced as rocks went where they weren't welcome but the pressing horror was the monster stalking in her direction. She started to crawl away, sweat and tears dripping down her cheeks, as the monster stalked closer. Despite its wirery frame, it walked like a dancer, confident in every step and graceful in its somewhat exaggerated movements.

It was nearly upon her, less than a pace away, when it froze. It growled in frustration as the lone ranger on duty, a thin man with a lanky frame wearing an ill-fitting green uniform and wielding a shotgun, ran to her. The ranger fired a single shot into the sky.

"Go on," he snapped in a heavy accent, "you know you shoudn't be here." Ashley watched the monster take a few steps away as the rippling air seemed to envelop it. In an instant, the monster was gone. The ranger turned to Ashley who was laying on the gravel, naked except for the tattered shirt and covered in blood that was mostly her own. "Are you alright?"

"What was that thing?" Ashley asked.

"Kids call it the Dracat," he chuckled "but I don't think there's a name for it."

"What?"

"They started calling it Dracula's Cat on account of its appearance, but they eventually shortened it to Dracat," he frowned, "It still sounds stupid." He held a hand to Ashley. "Come on, it can't get you here, it can't leave the forest." She looked to see a barely visible symbol carved into the rock so it could be buried under gravel without being damaged.

"You," Ashley gulped, "knew this thing was here and you let people come here?"

"It usually keeps away from people," the ranger said as he lifted Ashley to her feet, "unless they're being destructive beyond reason." He paused and looked at Ashley, he noticed that she was nearly naked aside from the bloodied shirt she wore, and gulped. "What were you doing out there?"

"My friends and I were camping." She thought about her lust for Richie, her love for Brian, and about her stupid rivalry with Stacy; the memories brought a tear to her eye.

"Camping? Sure." He laughed. "I'm sure that's what the Dracat thought you were doing."

THE WRAITHWOOD WEAVER
Thomas Lanthripp

I poked the campfire with a stick, wincing as the flames crackled and spat. We had been out here for hours. No phones and no electronics allowed at Camp New You! So, there was no way to see how much time had passed. The sun had long since set though, and the night only grew darker and colder.

Ava tightened her grip on her dark coat, her fingers pale, and her brown eyes flickered with the firelight. "Can't we head back to camp already? I'm freezing my..." Ava paused, glancing at the eerily grinning guidance counselor plopped on a log across from us. "...my uh, bottom off."

"Ava's right," I said, tossing the stick into the blaze and rubbing my hands together for warmth. "We've been out here just sitting around. Shouldn't we be heading back now?"

Bryce, sitting next to me, looked equally cold and miserable. I glanced around and noticed the other campfires a few yards off, at least five in total, each surrounded by clusters of campers. The whole camp was out here in the woods tonight, but for what reason, I still didn't understand. I wondered how many of them were as cold and confused as we were.

"You know what helps keep your mind off of things?" the counselor asked, his fingers tapping the rifle resting in his lap. "Good ol' fashioned campfire stories."

For wildlife, that had to be the reason for the gun I figured. Every counselor hauled one with them the past few days, never letting them go. Yet, despite the heavy set of arms, nobody, to my knowledge, ever saw any kind of wildlife around these parts. Not even a squirrel or bird.

"Really? I haven't heard one since I was a kid," Ava asked, her hands trembling as she fumbled around for a marshmallow in the bag crumbled by her boots. She picked one of the last from the bag and stuck it on a stick before holding it out to the fire.

"Better than doing nothing, I guess," Bryce mumbled, his breath visible in the chilly air. "Anyone got a good one?"

A few shuffling feet, nervous glances and nobody said a word. I watched the campfire nearby flicker, hushed voices drifting from the other campers. Their vague silhouettes moved in the darkness. I counted five other campfires, each a small island of light in the sea of night. My watchful gaze was broken by a hushed voice.

"I've got one," Matthew said, raising a hand. "It's about a camp cursed by a cruel and bloodthirsty monster. A camp full of teens who had no idea what they signed up for."

Ava raised her eyebrows, glancing towards me and I shrugged back.

"The campers were unaware of a certain legend. About the Wraithwood Weaver," Matthew continued.

"Wraithwood...like the Wraithwood around us?" Bryce asked, trying to scoff at the semblance of names but there lingered a hint of fear in his tone.

"Are you going to let him tell his story?" Ava asked as Bryce threw up his hands in defeat. Ava nodded for Matt to continue.

"Deep within the heart of Wraithwood Forest lives a creature known as the Wraithwood Weaver. The monster is rarely seen by human eyes, and those who do see it…they have nightmares of it for the rest of their pitiful lives," Matthew stated as his voice seemed to grow louder and echo around the forest. "You don't just find the Weaver…nooo…it finds you. See, it blends into the shadows and trees, never seen unless it wants to."

"What does it look like?" I dared to ask. Matthew cocked his head and matched my eyes with his hollow black ones. His face was obscured under a hoodie. The hairs along the back of my neck sprang upright.

"Countless stories describe it, each one a little different but they all share the same details. They say it's massive, bigger than most trees, and looks like a spider. Eight nasty, hairy legs that could rip a man apart in seconds. And don't even bother trying to get away, it moves swifter than a cheetah on those spiky legs. Just whoosh…and you're prey. Screaming as it plunges its fangs into you, oozing its concoction of acid, melting you into a nice human smoothie," Matthew made a slurping noise, and I shivered, looking back at Bryce, who pretended to yawn, but the hand covering his mouth trembled a bit.

"Seriously a giant spider that goes around hunting people? I thought You had something original, man," Bryce said, rolling his eyes.

"There's more to it; this isn't some ordinary spider," Matthew stated as he looked briefly at Counselor Jimmy, who still had that elongated smirk stretched across his face.

"The eyes are the first and probably last thing you'll see. Its eyes are heightened, though; they don't see just flesh and blood; they see your soul!" Matthew remarked as a gust hit and the firepit darkened for a second. "That's what it hungers for the most. Its monstrous claws are used not only for hunting but also for weaving webs that are almost invisible to the naked eye. But these aren't just any webs, they are said to be imbued with ancient magic. Magic that predates even humanity itself. Those webs latch onto the soul of the deceased before it's carried off. Your soul is wrapped up and stored for a hearty meal later.'

"Ew," Ava whispered as I nodded.

"So it craps your chewed-up soul out? That's messed up," Bryce snorted. The thought of being eaten twice by anything made my stomach knot up tight.

"The Native tribes spread the word and avoided the forest. And for the most part, the Weaver feasted on deer or birds, content until it met a new prey: Settlers. Wanting to claim the world, they tried to deal with the Weaver. Fire and guns, they threw everything at it…only to watch as the spider devoured them all. But…one settler did something different. He bargained with the spider."

"How the hell do you bargain with a spider?" Bryce asked as Matthew smirked, flashing a set of pearly white teeth. Some of them looked sharper than normal, but I chalked it up to the lighting.

"This particular settler built an altar and statue near the Weaver's hunting grounds. Brick by brick, he crafted it, and before long, he completed it. And that's where the story takes an interesting turn. The spider and man formed an agreement. In exchange for food, the spider weaved whatever the man desired with its otherworldly magic."

"I think this story has gone on long enough," Counselor Jimmy sighed and Matthew shook his head.

"Scared? It's just a story, right Counselor Jimmy?"

I half expected Counselor Jimmy to silence Matthew with his rifle at this point as it looked like the two refused to back down. After a minute, the counselor shrugged and returned the floor to Matt who eagerly continued.

"About three hundred years later, a group of teens spent the summer living it up near the forest," Matthew said. "Their biggest fear was getting caught drinking beer or smoking a little weed behind the tool shed."

"Amen," Bryce muttered, hands knitted together and head bowed.

"Four friends especially bonded over this little break. Practically inseparable," Matthew continued as I instinctively tugged on the rope bracelet the four of us at the fire shared. It was a piece of string to some, but to four socially anxious agoraphobes like us, it was a bond.

"Until the day came when the camp gathered together for a hike. Nothing unusual there, except the counselors started acting like they'd won the lottery."

"I'm not sure how I feel about this story," Counselor Jimmy interjected, but Matthew didn't seem fazed in the slightest.

"They walked and walked before they came up to this secluded area. The trail practically nonexistent," Matthew said, the memory of that lonely trail coming back to my mind. One wrong turn and it'd be pure luck if someone could find their way back.

"The campers, tired, got ready to set up for the night. One of them, though, noticed the counselors had left the kids alone. Ever curious, he stumbled off after them. And he found them…but it's where he found them that he realized the truth of this whole place."

"Mr. Edmond…I think that's enough," Counselor Jimmy's smile had disappeared. The two locked in a staring contest.

"The counselors had been whispering about the statue and altar for weeks, thinking the campers couldn't hear them. But one little camper overheard them. They were waiting for the perfect moment," Matthew said.

Counselor Jimmy's fingers drummed more insistently on the rifle, but he didn't interrupt. Matthew pressed on, emboldened by his silence.

"No one noticed any of this except for one camper. He saw the counselors feeding notes to a statue's stone lips.

And, as crazy as it sounds... the statue swallowed them. In their rush, one of the counselors dropped a note. The camper snuck back to see what that note said, and to his surprise, he found out the true horror of this little forest," Matthew said, pulling a scrap of paper from his pocket and unraveling it.

Ava's eyes widened and Bryce leaned in closer, both of their fear palpable. "What is that?" I asked.

"This handwriting looks familiar to anyone?" Matthew asked, holding out the small strip of parchment, barely the size of a person's palm. The dark letters were illuminated by the fire and it soon grew on me.

"Holy crap... that's... that's my mom's," I said softly, recognizing the slants and sloppy curves of the rushed handwriting. The kind of way she wrote when joy made her hands unsteady.

Matthew began to read the words aloud. "I wish for eternal life," Matthew said, pausing before the final part. "In exchange for the soul of my child."

"What the hell, man?" Bryce whispered. "This is some kind of a sick joke right?"

"I wish it was a joke," Matthew stated. "Haven't you noticed everyone here seems to have the best parents?

Getting you everything you want, and then the constant doctor check-ups?"

"Oh God," Ava's lip quivered as it seemed Matthew hit a sore spot.

I couldn't forget the trips to the doctor. The physicals where I'd be prodded with countless needles only for a clean bill of health. Mom always made sure I stayed out of trouble and ate only the best foods. And every day that I got older, she seemed happier.

"We're cattle, about to be delivered to the butcher," Matthew continued with a hint of a sardonic chuckle. "This camp isn't just a place for summer fun. It's a trap. Our parents sent us here to feed the Weaver to make their twisted wishes come true."

Counselor Jimmy stood, gun lifted, the fire casting long, menacing shadows across his face. "That's enough," he said, his voice low and dangerous. "You kids and your wild imaginations."

I hadn't noticed it at first. Distracted by Matthew's story I hadn't seen the other campfires start to extinguish. At first, it was only one, but soon a second and then a third vanished into the darkness.

"Oh my God...oh my God," Ava's eyes filled with water, daring to pout any second. My stomach tightened and I felt bile build in my throat.

"Matt...tell me this is just a sick joke!" I demanded as Matt stared listlessly into the fire. "Damn it, Matt!"

"It's not," Matthew whispered.

"We have to get out of here," Ava urged. "Before it's too late."

"I think it already is," I murmured, glancing nervously into the darkness surrounding us.

"You're not going anywhere, sit down," Counselor Jimmy ordered as the butt of his rifle planted against his shoulder.

"Or what? You gonna shoot us?" Bryce shot to his feet.

Suddenly, a rustling came from the shadows beyond the fire. The other campers' silhouettes grew dimmer, and before long, they vanished as the last firepit went out. From the pitch black, a low hiss emerged, sending shivers down our spines. We all turned away from Counselor Jimmy and faced the empty void. I squinted, praying for an angry badger or something.

A figure emerged from the shadows, dull eyes and limping. It was another camper, staggering around. He had a deep gash on his head and his shoulder was leaking red badly. Probably losing more blood than he should, yet we were all frozen to our spot.

"Please…he-help," The teen pleaded before a thin string landed on the top of his head. He screamed as the thread touched his hair and skin, and with a hard yank, he was pulled into the abyss. A single shoe flew off and remained.

"Run!" I shouted, grabbing Ava's hand and pulling her behind me. She almost fell, and briefly, the thought crossed my mind that if she did fall, I wouldn't look back. Bryce was right behind us, his face set with determination.

I turned to see if Matt followed in our footsteps, but he still sat on the overturned log, giving a pitiful wave.

As we bolted into the forest, the last thing I saw of the campfire was Counselor Jimmy raising his rifle, a grim smile on his face. "You can't escape!" The deranged man called after us. "The Weaver always gets her prey!"

The night closed in around us, and the sounds of pursuit grew louder. The creature's hisses and shuffling mixed with the distant sounds of the different counselors' taunts. But we kept running, fueled by the hope that maybe, just maybe, we could outrun this nightmare.

We sprinted through the trees, branches slashing at our faces and arms. The cold air burned our lungs, but we didn't dare slow down. Every snap of a twig and every rustle of leaves made my heart race faster. I glanced back once, seeing nothing but knowing if Matt's story bore any truth, by the time we did see something, it'd be too late.

"Over there!" Ava gasped, pointing to a faint trail leading deeper into the woods.

We veered off the main path, hoping the dense forest would provide some cover. The trees closed in around us, their branches like skeletal fingers clawing at the sky. The moonlight barely penetrated the canopy, casting eerie shadows that danced as we ran.

"Keep going!" Bryce urged, his breath coming in ragged gasps.

The trail wound through the forest, twisting and turning, disorienting us further. My legs felt like they were made of lead, but I forced myself to keep moving. We couldn't stop now. Not when freedom was so close.

A sudden cry rang out behind us, followed by the sound of something heavy crashing through the underbrush. I didn't dare look back. I just ran faster, my heart pounding in my ears.

"Look!" Ava cried, pointing ahead. "There's a cabin!"

In the dim moonlight, I could just make out the outline of a small, dilapidated cabin nestled among the trees. It wasn't much, but it was shelter. We sprinted toward it, bursting through the door and slamming it shut behind us.

Inside, the cabin was dark and musty, the air thick with the scent of decay. Broken furniture lay scattered across the floor, and, of course it had to be them, thick cobwebs hung from the ceiling. But at least it was a temporary refuge.

"We can't stay here long," Bryce said, his voice hoarse. "They'll find us."

I nodded, looking around for anything that might help us. "We need to barricade the door."

We quickly piled broken chairs and a rickety table against the door, hoping it would buy us some time. The sound of footsteps outside grew louder, and I could hear Counselor Jimmy's voice calling out, taunting us.

"Join the fun campers! Don't miss out!" The Counselor shouted as others joined in.

Ava sat huddled on the floor, leaving Bryce scrounging around for a weapon. Not that it'd matter. We had little chance against guns, let alone that thing. Our only hope was that we'd be safe here.

As we caught our breaths, Ava craned her up towards the ceiling. Her breath caught in her throat as she thrust a finger to the ceiling. I froze and looked up with Bryce. My heart almost stopped.

Amber eyes, dozens upon dozens of them, small and beady compared to the large orbs earlier, looked down at us. And then hissing, a whole symphony. And finally, I began to cry in horror as the creatures descended on us.

ISLAND OF THE MOGGIE
Ian Klink

"Though they may still be there," the bookseller started through rotted teeth, "I'd fear the madness those feral beasts become might have taken over the island."

Jameson pulled the cigarette off his dry lips, flicked the ashes, and spit upon their remains. "If I can get my hands on that book, then be dammed if they have become such wretched creatures."

The vagrant tilted his head back after inhaling, laughing like no other man Jameson had seen before. "Be brave, you are sir. The bravest of the finest men who have sailed around these parts in. every long time. Yes, indeed," he said through his laughter.

"Far from brave. Desperate," Jameson said.

"Desperate measures come from desperate times my father used to say."

"Something of that nature, yes," Jameson replied, tossing his spent cigarette on a pile of molded scout books. As the bookseller rushed to remove the fire hazard from his pitiful collection, Jameson placed another cigarette on his chapped lips and lit a match off the cover of a used atlas. "Why in the world would there be so many cats?"

"Some say it was his wife. She started with two, and well... A zebra cannot change its stripes. Neither can a horny kitty-kat."

Jameson just shook his head.

"Over the years they just grew and grew till there were some hundred cats they said. Some even say this is why they left the island."

Blowing out his smoke, Jameson cleared his throat. "Now, I hate to be persistent on this, but time is of the essence as I am most assuredly you are aware of.

"Yes. Yes, indeed," he said, wiping the ashes away.

Jameson pulled the envelope filled with three crips thousand-dollar bills and held it in the air.

The bookkeeper bared his toothless mouth, allowing Jameson to be disgusted by his two remaining rotted teeth, and reached for the envelope.

"No," Jameson quickly said, holding the envelope away from the old man's grasp.

"But you said-"

"I know everything that escapes these lips," Jameson coldly spoke. "Including these words, you are going to heed from. I have searched for this volume for so long that I have lost what is most dear to me sometimes."

The bookkeeper listened patiently to the madman's tale.

"What I hold in my hand is a promise. Not from myself but from you, good vagrant."

The bookkeeper just nodded.

"A promise that you are telling the truth. If this volume is on the island, as you have promised, then what I hold in my hand means nothing. Is there true understanding in the words I speak?"

There was a long pause from the bookkeeper. "No."

It was Jameson's turn to laugh. "Fascinating," he softly spoke.

"Huh?" The bookkeeper asked, whose hearing was worse than his dental health.

Jameson pulled the cigarette away and the worn smog danced as he spoke. "I use the word fascinating often when something intrigues me. If I had said the word interesting, it means nothing. Had I said interesting to you we would speak nothing between our souls, but since I uttered my preference, you should be honored vagrant."

The bookkeeper looked puzzled.

"Do not worry yourself. I do not expect a man who treasures trash to understand my intellectual verbiage."

"Sir I do not under-"

"Yes, yes, yes. I am well aware. I will ask you to remain silent while I explain myself."

The bookkeeper nodded his head, his bloodshot eyes never leaving the envelope.

"I want to make sure you understand that if what you tell me is the truth there will be a few more of what lies within the envelope for you."

"I am telling the truth. Inside the library on the island is the lost book you seek?"

"And what volume am I seeking?" Jameson quizzically asked.

Panic planted in the bookkeeper's eyes as he desperately searched the library in his mind till he found the answer. Saying the Roman numerals like they were spelled he yelled "XIII!"

Jameson smiled. "Very good. However, I want you to make sure that it is there."

"It was the last time I was there!"

"Pray tell, how long ago was this?"

"T'was fifteen years and seven... no five months ago. Yes, fifteen and five months."

The smile left Jameson's face. "For being so long ago how are you so sure!"

The bookkeeper backed a few steps away, unaware he was doing so.

"Stop," softly came from Jameson's lips. "I asked you, how sure are you it is still there."

"Because no one has been there since."

Another customer walked through the entrance of the shoddy storefront. "I will be with you soon," The bookkeeper said over Jameson's shoulder.

"No, he may not," Jameson said, never turning around. "This shop will remain closed for the rest of the day."

The customer looked at the bookkeeper for compliance, who only offered a shrug of his bony shoulders as the irritated person left his run-down establishment.

"Maybe you should place the closed sign up," Jameson suggested. "You need to tell me more about this island prison that holds my book."

The bookkeeper did as he was commanded while Jameson smiled, dragging the sweet nectar of his cigarette inside the temple of his body.

The steamboat he rented was still upon the waves as Jameson looked into the depths of the fog. According to the bookkeeper, he should have been on the island by now. "Bloody vagrant," he mumbled to himself, looking through the eyeglass towards nothing. "Captain Yates!" he yelled,

"Yessir," The steamboat captain answered behind the wheel, his glass eye looking toward the ocean.

"I don't see anything," Jameson spoke through his anger.

"I'm going off the coordinates you gave, sir."

Jameson turned coldly around. "If you want that pay, it would be prudent for you to correct this mistake."

"There is nothing I did wrong. Look at the dial! This is correct."

Jameson ran to the wheel and looked at the large compass on top. "This fog. Given how it appears right now, are you sure we are in the right direction?'

"Look, sir," the captain said, pointing his finger at the coordinates. "It is correct."

Jameson grabbed him by the collar of his peacoat and slammed him hard against the wheel. "Listen, you... you... scurvy hound!"

"Wait! Let go!'

"Where is it!" Jameson yelled, his voice echoing across the limitless fog. "Where the hell is the island?"

"I don't know!"

Jameson might have continued until the captain could breathe no more, but the screech of pelican made Jameson release his grip and ran to the edge of the boat, grabbing the engine wire to brace himself. "Where is that coming from?"

"There!" the captain said, pointing just off the front. "I see the dock."

Jameson smiled as the wooden dock appeared through the patches of fog. "Hurry up!"

"Yes, sir," the captain said, spinning the wheel toward the dock, splitting the fog as the steam bellowed out the top.

Jameson jumped onto the splintered dock and the first thing he noticed was the plethora of scratches across the top, especially the one near his foot. It was a fresh scratch, the wood lighter in nature, and blood was smeared across the four lines. "Captain Yates?" he summoned.

"Yes, sir," he said, tying off the line to the dock.

"You swear this is the correct island?"

"Yes, sir. It has been a while, but seeing this dock brought it all back. Yes, sir, this is the island Mr. McAree owned."

Jameson nodded and sighed. The reality of the volume being so close filled his heart with joy, but the island filled his gut with dread. "What make you of these?" he asked, pointing toward the scratches along the wood.

The captain stepped onto the deck and bent down, running his fingers along the scratches. "Moggies," he softly spoke.

"What?"

"Moggies. Cats... you know. Meow," the last part acted by the captain's best feline impersonation.

Inside his mind was a chuckle Jameson wanted to let out, but all he could do is stare at the blood. "What about the..." he trailed off.

"They have to eat, too," the captain said and laughed.

"What direction is the house?"

He peered across the dock through the gloom. "It should be that direction," he said, pointing. "If I remember right, and mind you it has been a while, the back doors were facing the dock."

"And the library?"

"Should be a few rooms down from those back doors."

Jameson took a deep breath and pulled out his Colt. He opened the chamber, checked to make sure the bullets were present, and slammed the chamber. "Alright. I will be proceeding to the house. I request you remain here. If the information you gave me is bound within truth, then I shall only be mere minutes, not longer." He leaned to leave and stopped. "The vagrant told me this island has been abandoned for some time. Is there truth to this?"

"No one has seen MacAfee on the main island in years."

"Does that mean he is still present? Or is he deceased? Answer me this?"

"I have no idea, good sir. I just know what I hear and what I hear is they are just gone. I've heard tails of looters who came to steal from the house. It is abandoned."

The assurance from the sailor did nothing to quelch his rising fear. "Then I shall find out soon. Remain here."

"Yes, sir."

Jameson nodded and started walking along the deck toward the house.

"Good sir?" Captain Yates called.

Jameson quickly turned around, the gun in his hand rising.

"Should you happen upon some canned food, I'd appreciate you bring some. I hunger like a lion."

Jameson spun around and quickly found himself lost in the fog.

Although dissipated of human life, the sounds of the island made Jameson aware he was not alone. Every step he took seemed to awaken some creature, excited for his presence and eager to announce the arrival to all who roamed. As he broke each small branch left over from some ocean storm, he could feel the new set of eyes staring at him, his shirt was wrenched with sweat and the fabric stuck to his back. Jameson felt the fog would have cooled him, but it added to the lunacy of this moment. As something cackled in the distance, Jameson froze when something fell to the ground from above. Waving the gun in the air, aimlessly pointing to nothing he could see, he felt maybe it had come too far.

Walking towards the discarded property, Jameson cursed his grandfather in the same sentence of his praise, for it was he who gifted the volumes to Jameson for his ninth birthday. Every day he took a few moments to open his Cary Safe, putting on the gloves to never soil their binding with his greasy fingers, to look at the volumes of the world's greatest horror stories. The kings of crimson death who fueled the nightmares of all who delve into their prose were represented in the collection. Picking up the first volume at the dawn of the day, Jameson had finished all of the volumes by the time the quarter moon gleamed into his windows.

Except for one volume.

There were twelve books in the collection, but his grandfather had lost Volume XIII

He was a careless madman! Stupid old fool! He had no right! No right to own such a collection!

His foot slipped on a rock and he stumbled, firing a bullet into the ground.

Jameson could feel the blood throbbing in his neck, feeling as if his heart would burst through the cavity of his sweaty chest.

"You alright, sir?" he heard Captain Yates yell from a distance.

Catching his breath, he summoned through a desert-dry throat the ability to answer. "Yes! Yes! Fine. I slipped."

"You want my help?" came after a moment.

"No! Stay!"

"Alright then, but be safe, good sir!"

Far off in the distance, something moaned.

It was soft and low, almost barely able to be heard by Jameson's ears. He pointed the gun in several directions, trying his best to protect from whatever direction the noise possibly came from.

It moaned again.

Something inside his mind told him to yell and he screamed into the misty air.

The moaning stopped, but worst yet was the silence that followed.

"Captain Yates?" he called.

"Yes, good sir."

He wet his lips and tried to speak when something snapped in the farness. "Are you still on the boat?"

"Yes, good sir. Have not moved. In need of service?"

He waved the gun in a circle, spinning as the fear rose from inside until the image of the lost volume squalled the irrational emotion. "No. But keep the engine on. I shall not be long."

"Will do kind sir. Will do."

Jameson slowly began walking again in the direction of the vacant home, his shaking thumb frozen on the hammer of the colt.

The brick steps were the first thing he saw in the fog and without realizing it, Jameson hurried his walk. He stopped when the second thing he saw was the bones. With a bug slithering across the rotted jawbone, Jameson bent down and used the barrel of his colt to brush the bug away. The jawbone wiggled enough to expose the left-over rotted meat underneath. The smell made Jameson back away and hold his nose.

Something hissed in the far distance, followed by the sound of something falling over and breaking.

The gun aimed in every direction he could, his finger sweating against the trigger. Inside his mind, he knew it would be doltish to fire, but his heart was in anguish from the dread lurking in the mist.

"Captain Yates?" he yelled against his better judgment.

There was no answer.

"Captain Yates?" he yelled louder.

Still no answer.

"Yates!" He yelled, cracking his vocal cords.

"Yes, sir?" echoed through the fog.

"Why didn't you answer?"

"Sorry, good sir. Was down below fixing a fishing rod. Thought we might like supper once you get the item."

Jameson, more relieved he answered than he would admit, nodded as if he was in front of him.

"Have you reached the house?"

"Yes. I am proceeding. Be careful," he offered, an unfamiliar offer rare of his character.

"Thank you, good sir."

Jameson looked down, kicked the used jawline away, and forged ahead, dreaming of touching the goat-bound binding of his beloved volume.

Jameson had been a brave man in his illustrious yet budding life. Having come from nothing, and striving to escape the nothing, he made himself a titan on industry before he turned the ripe age of twenty-two. He came close to obtaining the volume a few years prior until it was found out the owner was a liar, fabricating the story out of the need to extort from Jameson. A random bullet from a hired man's gun solved the issue of extortion, but never the issue of the missing volume. Searching the globe for his desired volume, it all led to Jameson walking up to the broken doors of the abandoned house.

He looked behind him before slowly stepping through the doorway, making sure nothing followed. Even though he knew Glass Eye Captain was the only one on the island with him, Jameson had the feeling he was being watched.

Maybe they are the eyes of the lord, judging me for my sin of desire.

He rattled the thought from his mind and stepped under the doorframe, a shard of glass breaking under his feet. He spun to make sure it didn't startle anything wondering.

There is nothing out there! Nothing! Nothing! Just get the damn book!

The instinctual beast inside him demanded he run as fast as he could, the calmer mind prevailed as he slowly walked into the hallway.

Like the bones outside that once were sheltered by the flesh, Jameson was walking through the skeleton of a once beautiful house. With every step through the tattered carpet, invested with mold and mites gnashing the threads away, Jameson could feel the sweat dripping down his back. He wiped it from his brow and realized for the first time the immense smell of urine soaking through the wood, the floor, and the pungent air. In his earlier years, he had visited a home for his sickly grandmother, and the memory of how it smelled arrived, unwelcomed, after each sickening breath. He turned around to walk out the door and stopped.

The volume.

It called loudly on his brain as if someone screamed it in his ears.

I must go on! I must have it! I must!

He spun around, pulled a handkerchief out of his back pocket, and covered his nose, the stench still odious through the barrier.

I must have it!

The vagrant had been correct. The library was only a few feet past the grand ballroom filled with moss, birds, and mold spread across most of the withered wallpaper, and as he stood in front of the door, lowering the handkerchief, he had to close his eyes.

For years he had only been driven by one thing, and all that stood in his way was the door to the room. He lifted the barrel of the colt and gently pushed the door open, ignoring the hundreds of scratches at the bottom of the door.

The sun beaming through the hole in the roof was enough to panic him. Although knowing there would be a broken window or two, he never imagined the books themselves falling victim to the island's wrath.

"No!" he heard himself yell.

In front of him lay a monstrous mound, taller than Jameson himself, of books, drenched with mildew, the pages warped and worn from the continuous stages of dry and damp. Among the books was a scattering of bones like he had seen before. Most were tiny, no more than the size of his palm, but the skulls seemed to have several sharp teeth, four longer than the others. Without counting, there seemed to be hundreds of these skulls lying next to the putrefied books.

It's in there!

He dropped the gun and ran toward the scattered library. Like a maniac in a ward, he began searching each sodden-bound book for the one promised to be there. Book after book, Bone after, bone, without remorse but fueled with anger, he threw against the decayed walls, breaking the walls further.

It must be! It must be! It must be!!!!!!!!!!!!

He grabbed a jawbone and sliced his hand. He screamed and hurled the bone across the room, breaking a glass vase that cost a fortune at the time. He buried his arms in the pile, lifting several books and bones, and threw them across the bowed floorboards, his blood spraying the surface.

Then his eyes came upon it.

Tales of Darkness - Volume VIII.

The leather-bound volume was dryer than the bones surrounding it. It had been spared God's anger for the island all these years. His collection was complete.

There were tears in his eyes, but he wiped them away, spreading his blood across his face.

Then he heard the growl from the corner of the room. It was hidden in the darkest part past the mound of books and bone.

Only the fear of what was making the noise could make Jameson take his eyes away from his treasure.

It let out a soft guttural heavy growl from the shadows and something rolled toward the mound.

Jameson screamed, for staring up at him with the glass eye was the head of Captain Yates, with half his jawline missing, and a large gash the size of Jameson's finger streaked through his eyes. A small droplet of blood escaped the veins still dangling from his ripped neck.

Jameson screamed and ran toward the door when it leaped in front of him. Frozen, Jameson could not believe his eyes, wiping them with his bloody hand for clarity.

It was a black cat, but greater than any he had ever seen. The stained broken claws made Jameson know this was what fed upon the scattered bones.

The vagrant had been wrong., The island had once been filled with hundreds of cats. All that remained was this hideous survivor with eyes of hatred and terror!

Before Jameson could scream the beast had already sunk its teeth into his throat, wrenching his neck clean off. As he clasped his gaping wound, he stumbled backward. Dying before his body fell upon the mound, his blood splattered upon the pages of his precious volume XIII and seeped into the cracks of its catskin leather binding.

THE CAIRN

Ryan A. Fleming

In the summer, the landscape was called majestic, but in the winter most of those same admirers would call it desolate. Michael Johnstone was one of those few who found more beauty in the desolation of winter than in what passed for summer in this country. One noticed the seasons far more distinctly atop the hills than at the elevations where people lived. People did live atop the hills once, Michael thought as he ate his lunch. It was evidenced by the small encirclement of weather-beaten stones that had once been the walls of someone's home.

He wondered how many people would have lived in that small hovel of stone and long-vanished turf. Two? Four? A dozen? Too many for any privacy, at any rate. As he finished the last of his corned beef sandwich and washed it down with a bottle of ginger beer, he wondered what compelled the former occupants of this place to vacate it. When he stood up from the little shelter, the full force of the winter wind began to beat him from behind, and the question was reframed in his mind: what compelled someone to build their home here in the first place?

Turning so that his back was against the wind he proceeded to fasten his waterproof jacket. His new stance brought something into his line of sight that gave him pause, oblivious to the chill that was creeping under his top layer while it was still unfastened. There was a cairn standing several meters from the ruined house.

He had not noticed it when he reached the house, which was perplexing as it lay in a direct line from the lowest ebb of the wall to the direction from which he had come. He would surely have had to have walked directly past it, or else he would have walked right into it. He shook his head; recomposed himself. Likely he was probably too cold and too focused on his destination to have noticed it. This thought spurned him back into action at refastening his jacket, then putting on his rucksack and tightening the straps, before finally putting his mittens back on over the bare hands with which he had eaten.

The cairn still held some mystery for him, though the stones that made it had probably been replaced and removed many times over he wondered which was there first. The cairn or the house? He would have guessed the house, but there was something about the cairn. The larger stones near the base seemed to be the same colour as those in the ruin, but surely people would be likely to take stones from the house and put them in the cairn. He himself picked up a stone from the house as he left it, a flat rectangular piece the colour of slate. It was traditional to carry a stone from the bottom to place atop the cairn, but he had long neglected such customs.

He placed the stone atop the cairn, regarded it for a moment as he could still not understand why it kept hold of his attention, and began walking back the way he came. He took three steps before he realised what his subconscious was trying to tell him. There was no snow on top of the cairn, everywhere else had at least a half inch covering it, including the house, where he had to wipe it off the stone he had chosen as his seat, yet there was not a single snowflake on the cairn.

After a single glance behind him, to make sure the cairn was still there, he doubled his pace and began his long walk back to the campsite.

**

The descent was always worse on the knees than the ascent, every hillwalker knows this. Michael could not say how much of this was psychological, the view of the ascent and the feel achievement at walking to the summit nullifying the effect it had on one's legs, and how much of it was genuinely physical, gravity bringing the whole weight down entirely on the knees on the descent. Most accidents, falls and injuries and the like, tended to happen on the descent. People grew careless thinking the worst was behind them; carelessness that led to wrong footing that led to trips that led to falls that led to broken bones or worse.

This carelessness was to be doubly avoided in winter. The snow changed the lay of the land, a crevice in the trail during summer might become packed with snow in the winter. A single step onto that snow could cause it to give way. The crevice would become a crevice again. The snow would go tumbling, taking whichever unfortunate soul had disturbed it down along with it. Then there was the ice, the water that trickled down from the summit in the summer along the trails could freeze in its tracks in winter. All it took was for a bit of snow to hide the ice and for some unsuspecting foot to touch it and its owner be sent careening down the trail.

Due care paid to what one was doing or not, your probability of having an accident lead to something worse was higher in winter because there were so few people using the trails and paths along the hills, glens, and lochs than there was in summer. All day Michael had not seen another single soul. This was how he liked it, for a man who found true beauty in the desolation of the country in winter the sight of other people enjoying it at the same time would have spoiled the scenery.

In the four days since he had begun this winter camping trip, he could count the other people he had seen on both hands. In most instances they appeared to be locals out walking their dogs or running an errand than people sharing his own enjoyment of the countryside in winter. In the years since he had begun taking these annual holidays his ears had begun finely tuned to the difference between sounds caused by animals and those caused by humans. The latter sounded clumsier, as though people would never think that their interaction with the land would have any impact beyond what they had intended. The sound of snow falling from a hundred meters back up the trail sounded like that – accidental, accentuated, and unnatural.

Michael stopped at the sound of the falling snow. A lot of it had fallen. Too much to have been caused by a bird or a rabbit or by happenstance. It would have to had been something big to have moved that much. A deer could have done it, but it was a narrow ridge and there was none to be seen against the white snow. He spun round, expecting to see someone further up the path. There was no one there, as far as he knew there was no one else for miles around. There was just the long trail of white broken occasionally by the browns or greens or yellows of the earth trying to break through.

He stared back for a moment longer, then took a deep draught of cool water from his hydration pack. The thought crossed his mind that he should stop drinking alcohol with his lunch while he was out walking in winter, if he was starting to hear things. Though he was sure he had heard it, he put it from his mind and continued down the trail.

***

When he reached his tent, it was already dusk – as well as early afternoon according to his watch. In the time it took to stow his kit in the tent, get a fire going, and prepare the stove to heat his dinner of vegetable soup it was already dark. While he sat on the little canvas seat eating the soup, he scanned his surroundings. There was no wind in the little clearing he found amongst the trees in the glen where he had made his camp, yet he could still feel the chill wind from the summit all around him.

Soaking up the last of his soup with a slice of bread, he finished off his dinner and set the pot down. Spinning on his seat he picked up a camp kettle full of water and put it on the stove, turning the heat back up. He turned on his portable radio, tuned in to a station that was playing something halfway decent, some long-forgotten power ballad from the 1980s, and turned the volume up.

He was not in the habit of listening to music without headphones and polluting the stillness of the countryside with human noise, but he wanted to shake the ill-feeling he had brought with him from the hill but did not want to tune himself out to the world with headphones – lest he fail to notice someone approaching.

As the high-pitched vocals of the lead singer of the unknown glam rock band were winding down to indicate the end of the song his kettle had boiled. He lifted the large flask he carried with him everywhere while camping and poured the hot water from the kettle into hit, to this he added two teabags, sealed the lid, and shook it several times. He then set it down on the snow to brew, wondering if he should have something a bit stronger to shake his foreboding. He had a half bottle of whisky somewhere in the tent to chase the cold away, purely medicinal he would have joked if there was anyone to listen.

His attention was caught by something, or rather the lack of something. Though the glam rock song had ended several minutes ago a new one had not replaced it. As he listened, he could not even hear the predictable patter of a radio DJ. A blast of static caused him to leap from his seat, knocking over both the seat and the flask. First time he had ever heard such a blast of static on digital radio.

In the glow around the snowy campsite by his fire he listened as a hoarse voice began to speak through his radio.

'Rochians! Murtherers! A daedna poach on the lairdskip! Let us be!' The voice from the radio said.

In the background of the voice there was a low cry as though from a child. A crash and a grunt silenced the voice. An adult's screams were added to the crying of the child. More rough grunts. The screaming and crying entered a crescendo and as the grunts retreated there came the sound of something wooden being snapped and pressed. The screaming subsided but the crying continued. Another, softer but still hoarse, voice came over the radio.

'Stap! Please!' It pleaded over the cries of the child. There came the sounds of slapping, which fell away as a new sound was added to the cacophony: a crackling sound.

The screams returned, louder, their panic had assumed a certain fatality. Soon both the crying and the screaming were lost to a series of coughs – one set hoarse the other soft and punctuated by cries. Those both eventually fell silent too, and just the crackling remained.

Michael had no idea how long he stood there listening to the crackling. He eventually realised he was listening to the crackling of his own campfire, unable to discern between the two. Realising this, he stirred, gingerly picking up the radio. It was silent, though it was still turned on and appeared to still be tuned into the same station he had listened to earlier.

He turned it over in his hands. He fiddled with the volume knob, but no sound came from it. He then fiddled with the tuning knob, and though the display lit up and the information changed there still came no sound. He switched it off and the information disappeared from the display. After considering turning it back on, he dropped it to the floor of the tent.

Moving quickly, he turned on all the lanterns and torches he had with him. Gathered the few objects outside the tent and threw them inside. The fire was soon doused, and he sat inside the tent with his feet sticking out and removed his boots. He took one last look into the darkness of the woods, before quickly zipping the tent closed.

He would have that drink after all.

***

He was being pursued.

Across a wild, frozen stretch of moor the thing chased him. He recognised this moor; it was on the route he had taken from the train station to his campsite the day he arrived here. The sky was bright, but there was no sun. The ground was white, but he could not feel the familiar crunch of snow under his boots as he ran.

He did not know what chased him, only that it meant him harm. He could not say how it began chasing him, only that it was. He risked a glance over his shoulder. It was closing the distance to him. It – that was all he could use to describe his pursuer. He saw nothing more than a black shroud, but it moved. Not just moved towards him, but it flapped, rose, and fell. It was like something unseen was under the tattered black shroud that marked its presence, and the shroud moved as it ran.

The thought occurred to drop his rucksack to run faster, but as he felt for the straps, he realised he was not wearing it. He tried to force himself to run faster. He felt odd; he was not out of breath. And he was not cold.

Ahead, he could see the path that led down from the moor to the road. The road led to the train station. He did not expect the thing to vanish once he reached a marker of civilisation, and he knew he could not keep up this pace all the way to the train station, but it was all could try. Perhaps a car would come along, however unlikely. He was almost there.

Closing in on the path that would hopefully lead to safety he felt a pull at his hood.

He did not stumble, but he turned his head and there his feet failed him.

Reaching out from the black shroud was a hand. Blackened, rough like sandpaper, five stubby fingers ending in long chipped yellow nails. It held his hood and now it reached out for his face.

***

His eyes opened.

The lantern he hung from the ceiling of the tent was still there, it was swinging slightly, the pale, yellow light emanating from it giving the shadows in the tent a pendulum effect.

He sat upright.

The tent was just as he left it when he finally gained the courage to go to sleep, it seemed not five minutes had passed since he wrapped himself in his sleeping bag. He unzipped the sleeping bag, slowly. There was nothing out of place, even the tin cup he had used for the whisky was still wet.

And yet why was the lantern moving? He thought.

He looked up at it, there was no sign of what had disturbed it. Could he have done it in his sleep? No, he could still only just reach it sitting upright by fully stretching his arm.

His deliberations were cut short but a loud blast of static from the digital radio, still by the tent entrance where he had dropped it earlier. Squirming out of the sleeping bag he crawled over the air mattress towards it. Lifting it in his hands he saw the display was still blank and the power switch still set to off. He struggled at the back to get the cover off the battery container; once removed he dug his nails in between the batteries and tore them out.

The static fell silent.

He stared at the radio; he was out of breath. As he panted, and his breathing returned to normal, he resolved to pack up as soon as the light outside allowed and head off. He would cut his holiday short. In the meantime, he unscrewed the cap of the whisky bottle and took a draught straight from it, the cup he had used earlier lying forgotten on the tent floor.

From the radio, the sound of a piercing scream filled the tent. It was inhuman, too high, too crackly. It was more like feedback, but there was unmistakably something conscious, and in agony, making the sound.

Michael clapped his hands over his ears and closed his eyes tightly, as though cutting off his sight would help dull the sound that was causing him physical pain.

After a few seconds, the scream dissipated. Shortly he could hear nothing through his covered ears aside from his own quickened pulse. Cautiously, he first removed his hands from his ears and then, after he confirmed there was still no screaming, opened his eyes.

The tent looked entirely normal, aside from the dropped bottle of whisky which would now give the sleeping bag the permanent smell of the water of life. Then came a rapid series of clicks from behind him.

The zipped entrance of the tent was slowly being opened.

Michael just sat where he was on the edge of the air mattress and stared. It moved slowly, but determinably. He considered for a moment that no one would unzip the entrance that slowly unless they were deliberately trying to frighten him, but that presumed it was someone human on the other side.

The shrouded, invisible figure that chased him in his dream flashed back into his mind.

The zip stopped a third of the way round the entrance flap. A hand reached in, the same blackened hand that had reached for his hood in the dream. It grasped the flap of the entrance, clearly in preparation of just ripping the rest of it open.

Having seen enough, Michael's body finally acted. He leapt to his knees and bolted for the entrance, hoping he might just knock aside whatever awaited outside the tent.

He did not look back as he felt the child of the air on him, nor the even colder snow on his bare hands, thermal covered knees, and sock covered feet. He sprang to his feet and began running.

He moved slowly, the combination of the cold and the fact he was trying to run through snow in socks. Soon those socks were soaked through as the heat from his body melted the snow that clung to them. But still he ran at the top speed he could muster.

The first light of the dawn was creeping over the hills that surrounded the moor, he was well past the trees now and he dared risk a look behind him. He was being chased across the moor by the same black shroud. He snapped his head back around and focused on where he was going. He tried to force his body through the cold, already it wanted nothing more than to collapse and begin shivering. In all likelihood, if he made it through this, he would die from the exposure of being outside in the snow in nothing more than long underwear.

Still, he ran. Determined to beat the thing that chased him. The thing that wanted to cause him harm. He was heading in the direction of the path that led down to the road that ran through the hills. If he could make that perhaps he might encounter a car along it. He ran as fast as someone could in his state of dress and dared not risk another look back.

He was nearing the path; he could see the slope down. Just a thin path down from the moor, with sheer drops on either side of it. He felt a scratch on the back of his neck, then a rough clutch like sandpaper being wrapped on his skin. He spun around.

He took a tumble, losing his footing on the narrow path, and fell from the sheer drop down the side of the hill.

It took only a matter of seconds from Michael to fall all the way. He was looking up as he fell, there was no shrouded figure watching him drop. Just a cairn at the top of the path, one that was not there before, or else he would have fallen into it.

There were rocks below the hill. He crashed into them without ever seeing them. His bones broke, but what killed him was one sharp rock where the back of his head landed. He lay there, spread eagled on the rocks. Eventually a passing motorist would see the strange white shape and investigate, they would wait until the emergency services arrived.

The spilled whisky told them all they thought they needed to know about how Michael met his death.

By summer, the incident was long forgotten, and those reaching the summit would think nothing of the cairn. People would take rocks from the bottom and place them on it when they reached the summit in an ancient tradition. Near the top was a sharp rock, with a faded, dark stain on it.

IT REALLY ISN'T SAFE OUT THERE
Ethan K. Lee

You look at Gwen's body and wonder whether burying the mangled corpse is good enough. You've heard stories of animals digging up rotten bodies—plenty of perfect crimes have been spoiled in such a fashion.

Sighing, you think maybe the better idea is to take her out to the middle of the lake. You can tie cinder blocks to her feet and then dump her in the center. Lakes are surprisingly great for disposing of bodies. Whereas the ocean floor might be entirely flat and clean, lakes have submerged trees, root systems, and even complicated caverns. Dive teams loathe lakes—it's too easy to get caught and asphyxiate.

You don't have cinder blocks, though.

Even if you did, it would still probably be better to cut up her body, which will take all night. Either way, you'd need to keep her corpse in the house for the day.

"No good. They'll come for it soon," you say aloud.

You check your watch. You've got maybe an hour before they come to retrieve Gwen, and as much as you think she deserved death, you're not comfortable with them getting ahold of the body.

Why not? It's not like she'd have cared if it was you or your sister, you think.

True, but that's part of it right? Even if Gwen never knows, at least in your heart, you'll always remember you were better than her.

Sweet.

"Shut up," you say.

You continue to just stare at the corpse. They brutalized her far beyond what you'd expected—eyes gouged out, breasts cut off, pubic area burned. There are nails in her thighs and ankles, as well as in her wrists. It looks like one of them had made an effort to decapitate Gwen but gotten too tired or bored to continue.

You have to get rid of the body. Fire will take too long and smells terrible–an acid bath is the best bet, but it's too complicated.

Fuck. Just make a decision.

You nod, then go to the tool shed to grab a tarp and some rope.

While you're sorry it's come to this, you think even Gwen would admit it was her own damn fault. Making friends with the creatures—what the hell was she thinking?

That you're a narcissist prick and there's no way anything in these woods is as bad as you claim

You smirk. "Well, half-right at least," you say to her corpse.

She doesn't respond now. Gwen's far less communicative given her current state. Only a few hours ago, though, she'd been full of righteous indignation.

"Come on. That's ridiculous," she'd said. You hadn't wanted to argue–Gwen was standing on the lake house porch in a white t-shirt that was turning ever more see-through from her wet body and a black bathing suit bottom so small you supposed she only wore it so that she wouldn't violate the town's ordinance on nude bathing.

Gwen had spent the entire day topless in a g-string on your boat—were you really going to spoil all that by arguing?

The answer had been surprising–yes. Yes, because there are some things in life more important than a half-naked beach blonde model willingly throwing herself at you. Yes, because no matter how good she looked, things like truth and justice are far more important ideals than the need for sex.

You'd put down your drink. Behind Gwen, Lake Caldwell spread out like a mirror underneath a cloudless sky. "It's not ridiculous at all. They're vicious monsters. Given the chance, they'd kill us both, mutilate our bodies, and drag us off as party decorations," you'd said.

Gwen had scoffed. She'd gone on and on at that point about how absurd it was to make such generalized accusations about a group of people. You'd bristled. You'd felt your heart thumping in your chest with the taste of iron in the back of your throat. Your family had lived on this lake for almost a century. Well, not lived exactly, not since your great-grandfather had left for law school in New York, essentially abandoning the cabin for fifty years. It had been your grandfather, along with your father's help, who'd returned to the cabin, brought in the architects to fix it up, hired an interior decorator, and gone through a decade of legal proceedings to remove squatters and all other claims to the property. Still, your family has been here for a long time dealing with the Outsiders, and for Gwen to pretend she had a better grasp of the situation was infuriating in a way that made your jaw clench.

If the Outsiders hadn't come, you might've bashed in Gwen's skull yourself.

"Maybe," you say to Gwen's corpse. You have her on the tarp now. The plan is simple: chop off the limbs and head, wrap each in a separate piece of tarp, fill the bundle with stones, tie it with rope, and drop it all to the bottom of the lake. You'll take the head inside. It's the teeth you're most worried about. Her fingerprints you'll singe off quickly with a knife heated over the stove, but the teeth need to be dealt with. You're not going to end up like those assholes getting thrown in jail over dental records.

You shake your head. "Nope. Absolutely not," you say.

You'd struggled even to comprehend Gwen's level of naivety. Was it the drugs? Was she honestly so secured and safe inside her cosmopolitan bubble that it was impossible to comprehend the idea that something horrific lurked in the shadows?

And so, despite Gwen's nearly naked toned body, you'd laughed at her naivety. "Then you go party with them tonight," you'd said.

For a moment, there'd been a look of hesitation on Gwen's face. Had she developed a small level of clarity on the situation? Had she made an honest assessment of what she was saying versus the reality of the Outsiders?

If so, it lasted only a minute. "If I knew how to find them, then gladly," she'd said.

"All you have to do is walk through the forest. They'll find you."

"I didn't bring hiking shoes."

You'd shrugged and then, in your anger, said the fateful words that had sealed Gwen's fate. "No problem. We'll have a bonfire tonight and see if they join us," you'd said.

Looking at Gwen's mutilated face now, you almost feel sorry for the trick you'd pulled. Had you thought they'd be this brutal with her? *Maybe. I'm not sure, honestly. Did I want her to die? I don't think so.*

Whatever you'd thought is now beside the point—you'd invited the Outsiders in, knowing they were ruthless and unpredictable.

Well, that's too bad now, isn't it?

Had you ever been such a naive fool as Gwen? Maybe as a child. Maybe as a boy of ten when you'd seen one of the Outsider children, its skin grey and flaking, its bulging yellow eyes staring at you from behind a tree, and you'd gone to play deeper into the woods thinking that this could be a new friend before your mother scooped you up in a panicked rush, screaming at you never to do that again.

No, anyone above the age of seven who looked at one of those malevolent psychopathic creatures and thought they deserved anything but to have a stake through the heart and their head on a spike was hopeless.

Hopeless like Gwen.

"I really am sorry it came to this," you say, and then bring the hatchet down on her left shoulder. Luckily, the blade is sharp. You make quick work of her limbs, needing to use a hammer to shatter the bones but otherwise working swiftly.

You check your watch. *Not fast enough,* you think. The Outsiders will be here in half an hour. You move to Gwen's head–Lord, is she beautiful. Yes, it's mostly silicone and makeup, but still, she is stunning. You consider putting it on display, if not in the open, at least in your bedroom back in New York. You could bring it down to Morris Taxidermy–you're sure Tom Morris would accept a few thousand to keep quiet about the pretty blonde head he was preserving.

You shake your head. No, you can't do that. You can't get sloppy or stupid.

Too bad.

By nightfall when you'd gotten the bonfire roaring, you weren't sure if Gwen had forgotten the argument or if she was too drunk and high to care. She'd danced around the firepit, giggling as the mushrooms worked through her system and the bottle of white wine in her hand sweated in the heat. You did your best to enjoy the evening, knowing as you did that soon the Outsiders would come, and Gwen's final party would be a nightmare.

"Worse than I thought," you say as you sever Gwen's head. It rolls to the side, the mutilated cheek where they'd carved a fake smile now glaring at you so you can see her back teeth.

It had happened faster than you could've imagined. One second, you heard rustling in the underbrush–the distinctive sound of their clawed feet padding across the dirt. Gwen had wrinkled her nose when she'd smelled them, but without any prior experience, with only knowing about them from the safety of the cabin, her mind couldn't process the danger.

Maybe something primordial in her brain, some primitive structure understood that the approaching creatures, no matter how similar to human beings, were in fact, enemies, horrific nightmares best to be avoided–but if so, Gwen ignored the warnings. She continued to dance, pouting her lips in your direction as she teased removing more clothes.

"If that comes off, you might as well be naked," you'd said.

Her eyes, pupils dilated to the size of quarters, had sparkled. "That sounds good to me," she'd purred.

You'd told Gwen you were going inside for another bottle, and she'd barely responded, just giving you a lazy smile as she continued to dance.

From safe inside the house, you'd watched through the back window as the Outsiders approached. Gwen saw them and recoiled. How could you not? They were vicious, disgusting creatures, horrific in appearance. Still, you'd had to laugh as Gwen had tried to regain her composure, clearly reminding herself how rude it was to judge a creature purely based on appearance.

She'd actually reached out a hand to greet one of the beasts right before it bit clean through her wrist. From there, the attack commenced with a practiced brutality that you'd found sickening but impossible not to watch.

You nod at Gwen's severed head. "Yes, darling. I watched the whole thing. I couldn't help myself," you say.

No, you couldn't–how could anyone turn away from such a spectacle? It was brutal and yet so magnificent because what you were watching was Hell on Earth; what you were seeing was the worst possible act that could be committed against a person. And there it was, right below, for your viewing pleasure.

You carry the packages containing Gwen's body out to the boat. Some of the blood seeps out as you walk down the dock, and you realize you'll have to pressure wash later. Worse, you'll need to clean the blood out of the yard.

Can't think of that now.

It's true, already, you've wasted too much time on silly daydreams. They'll be here soon, slavering jaws hanging agape at the thought of dragging Gwen back to their lair.

You once saw it, that place in the hills where they live, nothing but a dripping cave, unimaginably humid in the summer. Yes, Mom had told you to stay away, but how could you? So, you'd snuck away one afternoon in the woods, not really knowing where you were going, just following instinct until it brought you to their cavernous den beneath the rotted roots of a dead tree. It stank of carrion under there. The mud walls were hung with rusted shackles. Frayed ropes in the shape of nooses hung down from the tree roots.

And as you'd walked, knees trembling, delving ever deeper into their hole, you'd seen–

There's no reason to think of that now.

With Gwen's mutilated corpse safely on the boat, you set out for the middle of the lake. The temperature drops as you drive, making you realize you're still wearing nothing but a sleeveless shirt. Mom would've never let you out like this onto the lake, but Mom's not here. No, Mom's–

I said there's no reason to think of that.

The process of dumping Gwen's body takes about fifteen minutes. You drive around for another twenty, just in case any nosy neighbors wonder about the boat out on the lake so late at night. You doubt anyone will care. Gwen won't even be noticed missing for another three days, at which point you'll have her cell phone and car abandoned somewhere in the woods.

You slap your forehead. You should've saved some of her blood to sprinkle in the car. It doesn't matter now. You'll just have to make do.

It's two in the morning when you dock the boat, so you figure you can get about four hours of sleep, then pressure wash the dock and the grass before sending a few texts from Gwen's phone, pretending everything's dandy. You'll have to post to her socials, too, which will be obnoxious and time-consuming but necessary.

Walking back into the house, you smell the rotten scent of carrion and look to the tree line. You think you see yellow eyes glaring from within the bushes, but you can't be sure.

Yellow eyes. The same yellow eyes you saw under the tree. The same yellow eyes that looked up at you from above a drooling mouth while Mom–

"Nope," you say and head inside.

It's easier to breathe in the kitchen, and you strip off your clothes, only then realizing you've been sweating despite the cold. You need to shower. You need to sleep. All that can wait, however.

You pad noiselessly on bare feet to the basement door, then down the rickety old steps. Mom had asked your father to fix these, but he'd never gotten around to it, and then, of course, it was far too late. By then, Mom didn't care about broken basement stairs, and Dad was so outside of his mind that he'd have been useless anyway.

The basement refrigerator hums. Your heartbeat falls into rhythm with it. For a few precious moments, you just stand there, naked in the inky darkness, the cement beneath your feet cold and the dry, the dusty smell of the unfinished basement in your nostrils. You love it down here–always have. It's safe. It's calm. The walls are square and solid.

When your eyes adjust to the dark, you take a few slow strides to the refrigerator. It's amazing that, after all these years, your hands still tremble as you open the lid.

You notice Gwen's head first because it's the newest. The green eyes stare back at you, and you think you hear an accusation. It is as if she can't believe this is where you've placed her, that this icy tomb is to be her final resting place.

"Better than with them," you say.

Next, you turn to Candace, Joann, Neil, and Aliyah, checking to ensure everyone sleeps soundly. They all are–dreaming calmly in their refrigerated coffin. Aliyah is your favorite, and you press two fingers to her lips, mouthing that you still love her despite what she'd said. Finally, when you're sure the others are safe, you turn to Mom.

You want to touch her pale cheeks but resist the urge, knowing that it might wake her. You prefer to let her continue sleeping. "So beautiful," you say and plant a kiss on her forehead. "Safe. You'll always be safe."

VIXEN

J. Weintraub

I've always loved the wilderness, despite the fact that—or perhaps because of it—the most traumatic event of my life, up until now, took place there. It was in the North Cascades, just on the fringe of the national park, an area devoid of recognized trailheads and managed campsites, and all it took was a fearless and independent Scoutmaster, a handful of devoted Eagle Scout candidates, a moonless night, the need to relieve myself, a campfire burning down to its embers, perhaps a slip and a fall or a simple wrong turn and disorientation, and a day and a half later the silence of the forest was broken by the yelping of dogs and the drone of helicopters overhead. It became one of the longest search and rescue missions undertaken by the Skagit County sheriff's office, and even though the cadavers of two young men were found—one of them upstream a treacherous canyon river, the other downstream—neither of them were mine, and after almost three weeks, the effort was abandoned, and I was given up for dead.

It wasn't until almost the first onset of snow that I was discovered by a pair of hunters—Ian and Floyd--beneath a rock overhang, sheltered by a weave of twigs and leaves. My shirt, I was told, was held together with pine needles, my shoes matted with grasses and moss, and gnawed roots, acorn shells, and the bones of small mammals covered the ground around me. I was, apparently, too busy sharpening a branch with my Swiss Army knife to even notice Ian and Floyd as they approached.

I later learned that in the months following, membership in the Boy Scouts surged, and a survival group named a brigade after me. And yet I remember none of it. Absolutely nothing. Despite the entreaties of reporters and interviewers, I could not recall a single emotion I might have felt—hopes or fears—or even more material matters, how I found sustenance or sheltered myself. Not even the shred of a memory sufficient to fabricate the slightest of narratives. It was as if, rather than having fought daily to stay alive in the depths of a forest, I had been lying in a coma for weeks in a hospital bed, and then as soon as I awoke, whatever dreams and visions I may have had, no matter how vivid or deep, had vanished instantly like water through a sieve.

About all that I retained from my experience was, oddly enough, an even more intense attraction to the wilderness. The scent of pine and other natural life in the air, the crackle of dead foliage underfoot, the taste of berries and roots and other foods gathered raw, the flash of movement nearby, the songs of birds at dawn and the dead silence of midday, the streaks of pure color in the sunlight—as if from the broad strokes of a painter's brush—the solitude, the uncertainty, the primal anticipation of danger all seemed to hold me with an even tighter grip, and as soon as my divorce was complete, I closed on the Bradley Estate, a property at the edge of a deep forest on the downward slope just east of Boulder Springs, Washington.

Of course, that would have been the last straw for Dorothy, if the last straw had not already been laid down months before. I had been accused by my wife of "mental torment," although I assumed that was merely lawyer hyperbole for "incompatibility." In fact, the split had been rather amicable, with Dorothy getting most of our material possessions and with our financial holdings divided pretty much in half. I insisted on sole ownership of Wendy, but Dorothy had never been fond of cats anyway, and if, in fact, our marriage had lasted up to the move to Boulder Springs, my adoption of Vixen would have surely been another one of those final straws.

The Bradley Estate had been on the market for some time. The area around it had long been thought to be prime for development, but the recession earlier in the century ended all hopes for that, leaving behind several feeder roads heading nowhere and isolated lines of utility poles. Economic activity had generally been confined to the other side of Boulder Springs, with its vacation homes and resorts for skiers and hikers extending to the foothills of the North Cascades, although, fortunately, the Bradley Estate was close enough to town to have hooked up long ago with the its electrical and water systems.

Actually, the Estate was hardly an "estate," but rather a single dwelling surrounded by several acres of cleared ground that had once been a private garden. The building was basically one story with a narrow, peaked attic space extending most of its length. It stood on a foundation of granite blocks cut from a quarry nearby, but the rest of the structure was wood with a verandah sweeping around most of the exterior. Wide and long and flat, it reminded me, from a distance, of a huge river barge, and at its prow, it opened into a spacious reception area that funneled into a corridor with partitioned rooms leading up to the kitchen. At the entrance to the kitchen, where the verandah ended on both sides, two turret-like projections bulged outward, both with floor-to-ceiling bay windows. One became my dining area, and the other, overlooking the forest, became my office.

Attached to the stern, as it were, of the barge was what the realtor called a "bonus," a large carriage house that once had had access from the main building, but was now sealed up by the kitchen wall. Its windows were boarded, and the outer door, too, was sealed, although the realtor assured me that all I would need was a locksmith and a carpenter to convert it into a guest house, a garage, or an additional storage area. Later I was informed by the clerk at the grocery store that it once may have served as the final dwelling—or rather prison—of one of the Bradley children, a severely disabled autistic child with violent tendencies who had, apparently, lived and died there without ever having left the property. After his death, which was, according to the clerk, never reported, the family sealed the carriage house tight, and it has remained so ever since. "Of course, those are just rumors," the clerk said in reference to the Bradley kin. "And you know what rumors are, don't you? Just that. So many rumors."

The house was far too close to the forest for me to afford the insurance premiums, but, in fact, I did not intend to stay there for long. I was there to write, to finish the third volume of my *McElroy Murders* trilogy. I had already gone through most of my advance, and it was imperative that I submit a final manuscript before, as my publisher warned me, everyone had forgotten who both I and the McElroys were. I had no doubt that, given my isolation and lack of distractions, I could finish the book by the end of the year, and once prepub sales were in, I could determine whether I wanted to hold on to the estate—to write my next trilogy, say—or return to the city once and for all.

Of course, I could not spend all day, every day writing, and most of my mornings were devoted to hour-long hikes through the depths of the forest. It was at the end of one of those walks that I found Vixen or, rather, she found me.

The forest here was thick, dark, and ancient; it was also expansive and once it had climbed the other side of the slope across the river, it swept around Boulder Springs to join the wilderness at the foot of the mountain range extending west. Since there were no trails to speak of, I marked my progress on the barks of trees with the blade of my Swiss Army knife, which I always kept razor sharp; I was not about to get lost again, especially since, other than my cat Wendy, there was nobody around to notice my absence. I usually carried a camera with me, since, now that the construction crews were long gone, wildlife had returned in large numbers. Along with flocks of birds, both migratory and resident—owls, woodpeckers, falcons, and eagles--there were several varieties of deer, and even an occasional elk. As far as predators were concerned, I never saw anything larger than a black bear, although there were wolves, bobcats, coyotes, and others that fed off the growing populations of chipmunks and squirrels. Fortunately, at least according to the clerk at the grocery store, there had been no sightings of Bigfoot for several decades, although he did mention that a pair of wolverines had been spotted wandering around the lower slopes. "People on the east side of town," he told me, "generally do not let their pets run free," and although Wendy had access to an inner courtyard when we lived in the city, I decided then to keep her confined to the house.

I thought of those wolverines when, upon returning from one of my first hikes, I saw my front door shaking violently as if somebody, or something, were desperately trying to get inside. Approaching from beneath the verandah, I could not see what it was, so I climbed quietly up to one of the side entrances. When I turned the corner, I found a large feline scratching ferociously at the front door. Almost at once it noticed my shadow, but rather than flee into the woods as I had expected, it settled back on its haunches for a moment as if in reflection, and then arose and approached, slowly and with caution. Once it reached me, it twirled its body around my ankles, purring loudly enough for me to hear while I stood upright. Falling to my knees, I quickly learned that she was a female as I probed her softly with my fingers. I failed to find any tag or collar, but when she wedged herself between my thighs and began to purr even more loudly, I assumed that she had been someone's house pet, now lost or abandoned.

She was larger than the typical short-haired mongrel, heavily striped with those jagged lines zig-zagging across her face like tribal tattoos, and her brown, yellowish coloring probably camouflaged her well in the forest, for although she seemed to be hungry, she was certainly not starving. In fact, she was a good deal heavier than Wendy--who was basically the same species although she had a little Persian in her and a much thicker coat --and I wondered if there was a bit of a bobcat in this one.

"All right," I said, as she continued to snuggle deeper into my thighs, "we'll give it a try, but it's Wendy's call, not mine." When I got up, she followed me to the front door, and as soon as I saw the depth of the ragged furrows she had scratched into its wooden panels, I realized what her name would be, a combination of the feral and the seductive. "You're quite the terrorist aren't you, you . . . you little vixen?" She meowed and accompanied me into the house.

Wendy usually came to greet me when I returned from my hikes, but perhaps having been frightened by the scratching at the door, she now was waiting for me across the reception area, and as soon as she saw Vixen, her hair climbed up her spine, and she hissed. Vixen, almost as if she realized what was at stake, lowered her body and, slowing her pace to a crawl, began to slink toward the other cat. When she reached the middle of the room, she stopped, her stomach almost down to the floor. Wendy approached, they touched noses, and after she circled Vixen twice, Wendy raised her tail high and headed for the kitchen. The other cat, as if eager to be given a tour of the premises, followed, and shortly thereafter I joined them to open a can of cat food and to grill a hamburger for myself.

    From then on, the two seemed to get along, although at a distance. They never groomed one another, and Wendy chose to eat as far away from Vixen as possible. Wendy had her own scratch pole, too, and although I purchased an extra one for her new companion, Vixen preferred to concentrate on turning most of my second-hand furniture into sawdust. But from the time I bought a twin cat basket for Vixen and placed it near Wendy's in the warmest part of the reception area, they would often sleep together, although at night Wendy would sometimes settle into the cushions of the couch by my bed while Vixen prowled through the darkest corners of the house and into the most narrow of its hidden spaces.

I would also sometimes find the two of them sitting together, side-by-side, on the small bookcase in the reception area, staring out of the large picture window overlooking the forest, and on a few occasions, I was aroused from my desk by a howling cat scurrying and sliding across the floor. That would be Wendy, and when I got up to investigate, I would find Vixen still on the bookshelf, her tail swinging furiously back and forth, practically standing on her outstretched claws, scratching at the glass. She had probably seen a rabbit or some other small mammal crossing the lawn, but once— not very long ago--I was drawn from my desk by a vase crashing to the floor, and this time Wendy had run all the way into the kitchen to hide. The sun had already gone down, leaving the reception area dark, and when I turned on a desk lamp and pointed it toward the picture window, I found a pair of bright scarlet orbs of light flickering back at me. I had often been struck by the blank brightness of a cat's eyes suspended in midair like luminous disembodied buttons when struck by direct light, but they had always glimmered silver or white, never red, and I certainly intended to ask the vet about this oddity when I finally arranged to take Vixen into town for her rabies shots and to have her claws clipped down to the nibs.

That same night, I forgot to return the half-pound of hamburger that I had been defrosting on the kitchen countertop to the refrigerator before going to bed. In the past, such neglect had never bothered me, since I would be cooking the meat the next day, and Wendy never seemed interested in sampling the kind of food I was eating. But that next morning, when I awoke, only a few shreds of beef and fat, intertwined with fragments of plastic wrap, remained of my meal. Vixen was sitting at the far end of the countertop, contentedly licking her paws, as if in triumph.

Before she could react, I grabbed her, tossed her into a closet, and after slipping in a bowl of water and a small open carton of kitty litter, I again slammed the door shut. "It's solitary confinement for you today, my lady," I said in a voice loud enough for her to hear, and walked back into the kitchen to see if I could find anything else to eat.

Yes, I know. It's sheer folly to think I could teach a cat anything by punishing it at random, but not only was I very angry, I was also ravenously hungry. I had neglected to go shopping that week, and it was Sunday, and all I had in stock were a couple of hamburger buns, a box of crackers, a half can of coffee, and a moldy head of lettuce. A six pack of beer provided me with some additional sustenance but, in general, both Vixen and I went to sleep later that night on empty stomachs.

When I awoke the next morning, Wendy was whining outside the closet door and I had to lure her away with a tin of cat food. When she had finished, I cleaned out the bowl, filled it with the dry pellets that Vixen had always refused to eat, and placed it just outside the closet. "I'll let you out of solitary now, my dear," I said aloud, "but you're on bread and water for the day," and then I added, repeating what my vet in the city had once told me, "Besides, dry food's good for your teeth." When I opened the closet door, I expected Vixen to come plunging out in an almost invisible streak, but there was no movement from the inside, and as I bent over into the shadowy darkness, the sun rising behind my shoulders, to retrieve her water bowl, I saw only two specks of glittering red light, at eyelevel, staring back at me.

I have no idea when she finally left the closet, since I spent a good part of the day in town replenishing my provisions, and afterwards, I took a long walk in the forest, finally returning just before dark. I fed Wendy, but when I noticed that the bowl outside of the closet was still full of dry food, I said aloud, "I can be stubborn, too. That's all you're getting today!" I even expected Vixen to appear in the kitchen when I was grilling my hamburger. But I ate alone, and after a few hours of work on my manuscript, I went to bed.

I slept fitfully that night, awakened frequently by troublesome dreams, which I immediately forgot. But just after dawn I crept from beneath my sheets to find the house eerily silent. The cats rarely tried to awaken me unless I had been sleeping exceptionally late, but no matter how early I decided to get out of bed, I could usually sense stirring somewhere within the house. As I emerged into the corridor outside my bedroom, the silence seemed to deepen, although when I reached the reception area, I found Vixen sitting on the bookcase, quietly licking her paws. Wendy, her back to me, was still peacefully asleep in her basket. "Ok, breakfast, you two," but when I kneeled down to awaken Wendy, I noticed that the blanket beneath her was drenched in blood. Drawing closer, I saw that her viscera, mangled and gnawed, had spilled from an abdomen that had been sliced cleanly open from the sternum to her pelvis.

By the time I stood up, stepped back a few steps, and turned around, Vixen had disappeared.

It took me most of the day to bury Wendy. The grave had to be deep enough to protect her from the scavengers in the nearby forest but it also had to be wide enough to contain her basket, which acted as sort of a coffin. Wendy had been fond of her bed, but I wasn't burying her in it for sentimental reasons; rather, it was simply easiest for me to leave her where she was and wrap her and the basket up tightly together in one of the linen tablecloths Dorothy had left behind. And then I deposited my cat into her final resting place.

When I returned from the burial, the house seemed empty, and even though I opened up a can of her favorite flavor, Mariners Catch, Vixen never reemerged from the shadows that day.

By the next morning the bowl had been licked clean, and even though I refilled it almost immediately, Vixen remained secluded wherever she had been hiding. Finally, late in the afternoon, when I arose from my desk to make a pot of coffee, I found her sitting at the threshold of my office. She was staring up at me, but before I could make a move towards her, she fled down the hallway.

My writing had not been going well, and after brewing my coffee, I settled down in the reception area with an Elmore Leonard in hand to see if I could ease my mind. Vixen, always keeping her distance, was now intent on roaming along the perimeter of the space, as if she were searching for something, and I lifted my eyes often from my reading to watch her continue her hunt down the corridor and then through the partitioned rooms and finally into the kitchen. She repeated that same circuit over and over again, always, it seemed, with one eye on me, and if I stood up to refill my cup of coffee or even to stretch my body, she retreated quickly, as if she knew what she had done and feared retribution.

After returning to my desk in the evening, I soon found myself surrounded once again, by bunches of crumpled paper, and when I finally retired to the bedroom, I fell asleep sitting up on the couch, exhausted from my failed attempts to rekindle my imagination or to recapture the train of thought that had been disrupted by the events of the previous days.

When I woke an hour or two later, I found Vixen settled deep between my thighs, purring gently. I stroked her a few times, told her that "we needed to talk in the morning," and then got up to change. Once I had slipped between the sheets, she joined me in the bed, something she had never done before, as if she were now reluctant to leave me, although when I turned off my reading lamp and shifted to my side, I heard her drop to the floor and scamper from the room.

I again slept only until the early morning hours, and when I awoke it was to that same eerie silence that had disturbed me two days before. But that was understandable since I now had only one cat, and with her constant searching and wandering of the previous day, she was probably just as exhausted as I had been. So, I wasn't surprised to find Vixen still asleep in her basket, curled up with her back towards me. As I approached her, I made some clattering noises with the can against the porcelain bowl in my hand so that I wouldn't frighten her out of what appeared to be a deep sleep. But she didn't move. I bent down, and after I touched her shoulder, her body tilted slightly over, and when her head fell across the side of the basket, I saw that her eyes were wide open and that her tongue was dangling between her teeth out of the side of her mouth. As with Wendy, her intestines, also ravaged, were splayed across her sleeping basket in a pool of blood.

Before closing on the Bradly Estate, I had insisted that the realtor, at the seller's expense, hire the best extermination firm in the state to ensure that no vermin had since infested the property, and perhaps even more important, considering its proximity to the forest, that it was secure from all intruders. The last thing that I needed while trying to complete my manuscript was a family of raccoons or squirrels nesting and scurrying above me in the attic.

As soon as I had finished burying Vixen—in a grave right next to Wendy—I called that same pest control firm and it took almost every last penny I had in the bank to persuade them to come up from the city the following day for a complete inspection of the house. It was almost the same team from a few months before and it didn't take them very long to inform me that nothing much had changed from their previous visit. There was a new, small termite infestation beneath one of the verandah doors, and a few moths were found fluttering around in the attic—which they then fumigated--but other than myself, there was, they assured me, no other living presence inside the house. All access points were still secure, and nothing much larger than a mosquito could invade unless I neglected to close a door or a window. Before they left, however, I asked them to inspect the carriage house, but they insisted that any entrance through—or even under—the kitchen wall was impossible, and that since every opening on the outside of the carriage house—windows and doors, all of which had metal frames—had been soldered shut, they would need to demolish a portion of its structure to gain entry, and that they refused to do.

    Once they were gone, I grabbed the pickax from the storage room and brought it into the kitchen. When I reached the wall that separated it from the carriage house, I swung the pickax over my head. But after a moment's hesitation, I let it drop to the floor. I had decided to put the Bradly Estate back on the market as soon as I submitted my manuscript, and although I could probably count on loans from friends and further advances from my publisher to support me before the book was published, I certainly could not finance the reconstruction of a structural wall. I would leave it up to others to explore whatever mysteries lay within the confines of a carriage house under seal.

Before going to sleep that night, I left a half-pound of hamburger on the countertop to defrost. In the morning it was gone, the plastic wrap surrounding it torn into shreds.

The following day, I went into town to restock my freezer and pantry. The grocery clerk noticed that I had not purchased any cat food.

"They're gone," I said. "Both of them. Dead."

"Wolverines?" he asked.

"No. Something else. I buried them toward the edge of the forest. I think they'll be happy there."

"I'm sure they will," said the clerk. "Provided the Indian spirits don't mind."

"The Indian spirits?" I asked

"What, didn't the realtor tell you?" he replied. "That's sacred ground out there, or at least some people think it is. Chinook, where some of their most heroic and savage warriors were said to be buried long ago. On certain nights, drums have been heard beating just beyond the forest wall. Haven't you heard them?"

"Drums?" I asked.

"Or maybe they're just woodland noises. You never know about these things, do you? Drums. Bigfoot. Noises. Rumors. Just so many rumors. . . . By the way, not to seem too nosey, but you sure like your hamburger, don't you?"

I smiled weakly and nodded, having no desire to tell him that I had lost much of my appetite and that most of the hamburger was not for me.

I began leaving a half-pound out every other night, and by morning, it was always gone.

One night I stayed awake, sitting in one of the kitchen's shadowy corners, with a gun in hand, but whatever was eating my hamburger seemed to sense my presence, and the meat remained on the countertop untouched until I slipped it back into the refrigerator and I finally went to bed. On another night, I fell into a deep sleep on the stool right there next to the pantry; when I awoke several hours later, oddly enough, I was lying prone on top of my blanket and, of course, upon my return to the kitchen, except for some remnants left behind, the countertop was empty.

I suppose that most reasonable people under such uncertain circumstances would have long since departed for somewhere else. But I've pretty much run out of money, and where could I go? Besides, I was still comfortable writing in my office there, and my work was again producing good results. During the day, even as winter approached, I had lengthened my walks in the forest, but since I continued to have difficulty sleeping, I often wrote deep into the early morning hours. In fact, as long as I left my offering on the kitchen countertop every other night, I did not feel especially threatened. . . until about a month ago.

That morning, when I awoke, I found the walls and floor of the kitchen splattered with fragments of the meat I had left out, as if the package had exploded or, rather, been shredded before being devoured in a fit of violent rage. Two nights late, I increased the portion by a quarter pound, and in the morning, everything had returned to normal, with only a few grease spots left behind.

I'm now working on my last two chapters, but I haven't really revised very much, and I fear that the entire manuscript will require significant and lengthy editing before I can submit it. Ordinarily, this would be normal practice for me and not much of a concern, but just the other morning, I again woke to a find a portion of my offering sprayed across the kitchen with even more fury than before, the floor slippery with fat, the ceiling dripping with meat. The next night I left a full pound out, and in the morning I needed to do no more than wipe the countertop clean with a few swipes of my sponge.

Since then, I've transferred my nine-millimeter Glock pistol from the drawer of my night table to beneath my pillow when I go to sleep and I have also begun to cuddle up in bed with a loaded, shotgun by my side, which, by the way, I've named Dorothy. I realize that, even with such armament, I would have little chance against something that could pounce upon two sleeping cats and eviscerate them without them hardly stirring. But still, I find the Glock and Dorothy to be comforting, and they help me to sleep, although I am becoming increasingly concerned that whatever it is that I am feeding in my kitchen every other night seems to be getting bigger and growing hungrier.

THE WRONG TURN
Michael Castillo

Still fueled by adrenaline from the concert they had just attended, the three young girls slowly embarked on the journey back home. With their ears still ringing, they smiled and joked around as they merged onto the crowded expressway. Once a beacon of speed, the expressway had transformed into a parking lot with bumper-to-bumper traffic. Brake lights stretched out before them like a vast sea of burning red eyes. The air was thick with the scent of exhaust and the hum of idle engines. The concert had ended late, and the small-town girls were exhausted and ready to get back home. Jessie, Kelly, and Zoe had all piled into Jessie's older-model Volkswagen Beetle and traveled a little more than a hundred miles to see their favorite artist perform.

"It's going to take forever by the time we get home," Kelly said as she sat in the passenger seat, playing on her phone. With sparkling green eyes and golden locks of hair to match, it came as no surprise that the 21-year-old was always the most popular of the three.

"Yeah, but it was so worth it. That show was amazing," Zoe exclaimed from the back seat, her hands fumbling around on her phone as well. Her chestnut-colored eyes were locked in, focused on the pics and videos that she had recorded of the concert earlier. She had been best friends with the two girls ever since high school. Tall and athletic, the caramel-toned young girl was an avid competitor in track, often placing as one of the top finalists.

"As bad as this traffic is, it's going to take us forever," Jessie chimed in while she blasted the horn, adding to the restlessness in the air. The oldest of the group by a couple of years, Jessie was looked upon as an older sister by her two friends. With dazzling ocean-blue eyes and sun-kissed skin, the raven-haired beauty sighed and threw the car into park. With the freeway as gridlocked as it was, she realized that they weren't going anywhere anytime soon.

Some time had passed, and frustration and boredom started to set in. The girls' lively and energetic chatter had slowly began to dwindle the longer they sat in one spot.

"Hey, how much longer is it until our exit comes up?" Jessie inquired while shifting the old Beetle into gear just long enough to travel a few feet.

"Let me check," Kelly said as she pulled up the GPS on her phone. Her nose wrinkled, and with a grimace on her face, she answered, "Bad news. We're not even close to it."

"There's got to be another way around," Jessie exclaimed. "I think I'm going to take this upcoming exit and figure something out."

"Are you sure? We don't know our way around here."

"Kelly's got the GPS; it's just a slight detour... relax," Jessie said as she spotted an exit sign, beckoning her escape. Desperate to get home, Jessie made the split-second decision to abandon the freeway. She threw the car into gear and steered off into the relative unknown, leaving the frustrating crawl of traffic behind. Their spirits lifted as they raced down the busy roadways of the city. Towers of glass and steel were a welcoming sight, as were the partially empty streets. The warm, incandescent glow of storefronts and streetlights paved their path as the girls navigated further into the city.

After a while, as the night marched on, the sea of red light faded into the distance. The bright, neon business signs that had lined the streets were now absent from view. The once-bustling city streets seemed eerily quiet. As the three girls continued, they noticed that more and more buildings and stores were closed and boarded up. The neighborhoods they passed through were neglected and appeared destitute in comparison to where they had come from. Unaware of their surroundings, it was clear that they had strayed far from their intended exit.

"Hey guys, I think we're lost," Jessie remarked. "That last turn you told me to take, Kelly, just led us further away."

"Hey, it's not my fault. It's my phone, Jess; it's having trouble getting service," Kelly said as she waved the phone around in hopes of getting a better signal.

"What about your phone, Zoe?"

"Sorry, ladies. My phone died about thirty minutes ago. Between the videos at the concert and posting and sharing them online, the battery ran out," Zoe said while holding her phone up, showing everyone a blank screen. "Maybe if somebody had a phone charger in this old, outdated car, then I could charge it."

"Hey, now. I'll have you know my car isn't old," Jessie said quickly, defending her car. "It's a vintage collector's car."

The girls chuckled at the remark as Jessie turned down a darkened street. The streetlights that lined the road were either mostly burned out or malfunctioning, which caused them to flicker. Jessie figured that she was better off using her phone since everyone else's phones weren't working. She fumbled around in the dark for her phone while her other hand gripped tightly around the steering wheel. Her attention shifted back and forth from the dark, empty streets to the lock screen on her phone.

The old Beetle jolted as it hit an unseen pothole in the middle of the lonely street. The unexpected movement caused Jessie's phone to slip from her hand and fall onto the floorboard. The phone landed precariously between the gas and brake pedals, making it difficult to find in the dark. Jessie took her eyes off the road for a brief second—focusing her attention on quickly trying to recover the doomed phone. As the car accelerated, she never saw the silhouette of a lone figure cross the street in front of her. She never saw her headlights reflected off the metal shopping cart that the figure pushed around.

"Look out!" Zoe screamed as the car hit the figure head-on. The force of the impact shook everyone in the car, bringing their collective attention to the scene unfolding before them. The windshield cracked with a deafening force as the figure's body smashed into it and rolled over the car. His body slammed onto the pavement with a lifeless thud. Everything happened in a split second, leaving the three girls reeling in shock. The smell of burnt rubber filled the night air as the car's tires came to a screeching halt. Jessie stared, horrified, at the cracked windshield, her hands still tightly gripping the steering wheel. Broken glass and specks of blood were all that met her frightened gaze in return.

"Oh my God, we just hit someone!" Kelly exclaimed, frantically looking around.

"Is everyone okay?" Jessie asked, her complexion pale as a ghost, and a sense of dread fluttered in her stomach. The other girls nodded their heads to indicate that they were unharmed. A few feet from them, the twisted frame of the shopping cart lay on its side, its rear wheel still spinning from the impact.

"I'm going to see if that person needs help," Kelly said as she exited the car.

"Just be careful. I'm going to try to call 911," Jessie remarked. Her hands trembled as she tried to get a signal to make the call. In the backseat, Zoe looked on with bated breath as Kelly exited the car and made her way over to investigate.

In the middle of the dimly lit, empty street, the figure of what appeared to be a man lay stretched out across the pavement. In the dark, it was hard to make out anything about the man except for his tattered and worn attire. His body slowly began to move and stir to life as Kelly inched her way closer. She called out to see if the man needed any help but received no response. Her heart raced with anticipation the closer she got. Jessie continued trying to reach emergency services, but her phone kept having issues connecting to the service.

Slowly, the figure rose, his movements slow and staggered. Kelly stood a couple of feet behind him, still offering help. He gradually turned around and focused his attention on the young girl. His hair, long and unkempt, obscured most of his face except for the stoic man's piercing eyes. Dressed in rags, his eyes stared at the girl with a murderous rage—a rage that burned behind pupils as dark as night.

"Oh my God! Are you okay?" Kelly exclaimed as she reached out to see if the man needed anything. "We never saw you, mister. My friends are calling for help right now. Maybe you should sit down or something."

The ragged figure said nothing, his brows furrowed and eyes narrowed. A sinister smile danced across the man's bloodied lips as blood oozed from his mouth. Slowly, he straightened his posture to a more dominant stance. His hand ran down the seam of his tattered black coat, parting it to the side to reveal a large fireman's ax tied to his waist. The ax was worn and old, much like the man who brandished it, held to his slim waist by a piece of filthy leather strapping.

Kelly froze in terror as the derelict stranger raised the ax high above his head. Her body screamed for her to move, to run as fast as her long legs would carry her, but she couldn't move. Paralyzed with fear and weighed down by terror, she could only stand there and watch her demise. For a split second, the blade of the ax gleamed in the moonlight. The silver metal sparkled with brilliance as it reflected the glow of the moon above. Kelly gasped in shock as the axe swept down, swishing audibly through the air, penetrating deeply into her skull. The noise it made was similar to that of a walnut being cracked open. She collapsed. Her body fell limp onto the pavement as if all her muscles had given out.

Zoe was the first to lay eyes on the ragged man as she glanced up, seeing his reflection in the rearview mirror. She stared in disbelief, her eyes straining against the darkness to make out what she was witnessing. The Ragman stood towering over Kelly's body as it twitched with an involuntary muscle spasm; the last little bit of life in her still fighting to flee. His expression was twisted into a cruel smile as he watched her succumb to his brutality.

"Kelly!" Zoe screamed.

Jessie's heart stopped as she looked up and saw the lifeless body of her best friend, slain on the pavement. Her phone fell from her trembling fingers back onto the darkened floorboard of the old car. Dread washed over the two girls as they frantically began to panic.

"He just killed her!"

"We have to get help," Jessie exclaimed as she tried to start the car.

"We can't just leave her," Zoe said as she crawled over to the front seat while locking the doors. Her tear-filled eyes watched as a cloud of red mist sprayed the air when the Ragman ripped the ax from the base of her friend's skull.

"Come on," Jessie said, abandoning the old car. "We have to move. I can't get the car to start. We'll come back for help. I promise."

Desperate to escape, the girls exited and ran off into the dead of night, leaving their phones and the old car behind. Guided only by poorly illuminated streetlights, they raced to put distance between themselves and the killer. Down the desolate streets they ran, where the silence was deafening and the path was unfamiliar. The only sound was the wild thumping of their own hearts and the echo of their footsteps on the pavement. Their breath came out in frantic gasps. Every shadow seemed to hold a potential threat—every sound was the sound of their pursuer closing in.

As the night waned, the girls realized that they still had no clue as to their whereabouts. Every street was empty, and every corner led to another dead end, leaving them feeling increasingly lost and disoriented. Tired and out of breath, the girls decided to cut through a relatively dark alley to rest. Jessie figured it would be a good place to keep out of sight. At the end of the graffiti-ridden alley, a chain-link fence separated it from the rest of the street.

"Do you think we lost him?" Zoe inquired while catching her breath.

"I don't know. We haven't seen him for a good while."

"None of this would've happened if you had just stayed on the goddamn road. We would've been home by now, and Kelly... Kelly would still be alive," Zoe said, her tone firm and direct.

"I'm sorry. I've been thinking about that ever since I saw her body lying there. She was my best friend too," Jessie said, still out of breath. "And now I've got to live with that guilt."

Jessie walked over and looked to the other side of the chain-link fence. Wooden pallets and empty boxes littered that side of the fence. Abandoned in the corner was a spool of razor wire fencing surrounded by trash. More importantly, off in the distance, she could make out the bright glow of a neon sign.

"Hey," Jessie said while looking for a way around or through the fence, "look over there. It looks like there's a 24-hour open sign a couple of blocks that way. Maybe there's a store or somewhere we can get some help. We just need to get around this fence."

"Shh... Did you hear that?" Zoe asked as she stared at the end of the long alley. In the faint distance, she could hear a harsh, grating noise that made her wince, similar to nails on a chalkboard but deeper and more menacing. The sound was a mixture of a high-pitched squeal quickly followed by a lower, grinding rumble, as if metal were being dragged along a rough surface. With every passing second, the sound grew closer, louder, and more defined. Fear swept in like a rushing river when Zoe realized that what she was hearing was the sound of an ax being dragged across the pavement.

"Oh God, he's here," Zoe said, her voice edged with terror as the two froze where they stood and stared at the end of the alleyway. Through the darkness, they could barely make out the silhouette of a shadowy figure slowly approaching. The sound of his blood-soaked ax ominously dragged behind him as he inched his way closer. The Ragman said nothing—he didn't need to. The sound of his ax trailing behind was all that he needed. With maniacal focus, he marched closer, always shrouded by the shadows, his face obscured as if even the light cowered away from him. Heart racing, Zoe exclaimed, "We need to find a way out of here. Fast."

"Over here," Jessie said as she knelt by a corner of the fence. "There's a weak spot here that I think we could get through. I'll go first."

Jessie frantically began to peel back a small section of the fence. Her fear spiked, and her heart pounded as she managed to create a gap large enough to crawl through. Her petite frame allowed her to slip in with ease. As she crawled to the other side, her leg caught on a jagged piece of the fence, leaving a deep gash in her supple flesh. Ignoring the excruciating pain, she gritted her teeth and pushed herself to the other side. All the while, the maddening sound of the ax dragging on the ground drew closer.

Without hesitation, Jessie bolted up and held the jagged corner of the fence for her friend to safely crawl under. As Zoe made it to the other side, the two girls came face-to-face with their pursuer. The Ragman stood alone and undaunted, his menacing stare penetrating as he looked at the two girls. The cold glint in his eyes and the sinister smile that traced the lips of his drawn face radiated an aura of malevolence and cruelty that sent a terrible shudder through the girls' bodies.

Hoping to deter him, they knocked over what they could find, blocking the path in the fence. Boxes and wooden pallets toppled over as they scrambled across the barren street, their goal in focus just a couple of blocks away.

The neon glow of the convenience store sign was like a beacon of hope and salvation. A wave of relief washed over the two girls as they entered the brightly lit store. The store was deserted at this time of night, except for the young store clerk behind the counter. Looking worse for wear as they came in, the clerk stared in dismay at the two girls.

"Please, you've got to help us," Zoe said, her voice thick with desperation as she and Jessie collapsed to the floor, their bodies exhausted and fear-stricken. The store clerk, a young man in his early twenties, rushed over to them, concern etched on his face. His eyes widened as he took in the sight of the two girls, clearly shaken and in great distress. He immediately asked if they had been in an accident or if they needed any help. The two girls nodded weakly; relief flooded their faces as they began to tell the clerk about the events of that night.

"I called the police. I'm not sure how long it's going to be until they get here, though," the young clerk said. "Traffic is still pretty backed up, but you two are welcome to stay here as long as you like. Hardly anyone comes into the store this late at night. I'm Trevor, by the way."

Jessie thanked him for his kindness as she carefully bandaged her injury. The wound was quite deep, and she knew that she would require stitches for sure. Meanwhile, Zoe nervously paced back and forth in the deserted store, anxiously awaiting the arrival of the police. Trevor locked the front doors, hoping to ease their worries somewhat. He was tall and slim-built, with densely coiled black hair and a distinct Detroit accent. Underneath his tough exterior, he came across as a genuinely good-hearted person. While they waited, the three of them engaged in small talk to help pass the time.

Suddenly, the lights went off, and everything powered down, plunging the store into total darkness. Immediately, Jessie and Zoe began to panic, their minds racing with rising fear as they dreaded the worst. Trevor was quick to console them by telling them that the backup power would kick on at any minute. Within seconds, the electric hum of the emergency lights powering on filled the store. Most of the store returned to full power, except for a few flickering overhead lights. It was enough to put their fears to rest, if only for a short while.

"Hey," Trevor said, getting the attention of the two girls. "Is the guy who was chasing you wearing an old, dirty coat, long hair, and a creepy smile?"

"Yeah... how did you know that?"

"Because he's looking right at us," Trevor said while motioning toward the front door. Jessie and Zoe froze where they stood, their hearts sinking to the pits of their stomachs. Like an agent of death, the cold-blooded killer stood at the front door, his determination unwavering. He gently tapped the bloodied ax against the glass door as he leaned in to gaze inside. A set of unsightly yellow teeth peered out as he menacingly smiled.

"We're closed tonight, asshole," Trevor remarked as he stood steadfast with his fists balled up.

"It must've been him who cut the power off." Jessie said as she quickly scrambled to her feet, her heart still racing with fear.

"We can't leave; the police will be here any minute," Zoe remarked. "I think I might have an idea. If you can distract him, I'll go out the back door, run around, and get his attention. You're not going to be able to run for long with your leg in that condition. And you know I'm fast—I can do this. I can buy us some time until help arrives."

Jessie reluctantly agreed to the idea and started to make noise in hopes of getting the Ragman's attention. The lights began to ominously dim and flicker as the store tried to keep up with the emergency power's backup. Jessie began to holler and pound on the metal shelves to draw his attention. Each thud echoed through the empty aisles, intensified by her fear and urgency. The doors rattled as he violently shook them in a failed attempt to get inside. His hollow eyes surveyed the store, pausing for a moment. With a cruel smile, he said nothing, backed away from the doors, and retreated out of sight into the shadows.

As Jessie caused a diversion at the front of the store, Trevor and Zoe swiftly made their way toward the rear exit. The young girl's senses were heightened, and her pulse raced with wild anticipation. Zoe took a few deep breaths and closed her eyes in an effort to compose herself. She nodded to Trevor to open the door. As he turned the doorknob, an overwhelming rush of excitement and dread surged through Zoe's veins. The door creaked open, and she bolted through the opening, propelled by an adrenaline-fueled determination.

Unbeknownst to her, a strand of razor wire fencing had been strategically placed outside the door—a trap meticulously crafted by the Ragman to inflict cruelty and pain. She never saw the thin metallic wire until it was too late. Her eyes widened as she saw the glint from the dimly lit streetlight reflected off the razor-sharp wire at the last second. In an instant, the barbed wire tightened, clotheslining her as it sank its metal teeth into her skin. Pain coursed through her as the razors dug deep into her throat, their serrated edges slicing through flesh and sending a spray of crimson into the air. Zoe's body collapsed to the hard ground like a marionette with severed strings.

"Oh God!" Trevor exclaimed, paralyzed with fear.

Trevor's heart stopped as he watched in horror as Zoe lay on the floor, gasping for precious breath. The steel wire, like a silent assassin, had viciously punctured a vital artery in her neck. The metallic scent of blood, combined with a desperate gurgling sound, filled the night air. Trevor rushed over to her in a panic and knelt beside her struggling body. His hands trembled as he wrapped them around her throat, desperate to slow the flow of blood as it poured out, staining the cold pavement below.

"Trevor!" Jessie screamed, "Look out!"

The tall, thin vagrant stood at the doorway with an ominous presence. His disheveled hair hung loosely around his face, partially shrouding his hard, piercing eyes and menacing sneer. The Ragman's hands gripped tightly around his ax as he took a step forward toward them. Trevor watched in horror, helpless to do anything as life gradually slipped away from Zoe. The air felt suffocating, as if every breath he took had turned toxic. The young man felt an intense rage swell up within him; his muscles tensed, and his fists clenched.

In an instant, Trevor lunged at the Ragman as he swung his ax and missed. He toppled the deranged stranger with ease, pinning him to the ground. Jessie was frozen with a mixture of terror and relief as she watched Trevor relentlessly pummel the killer with a barrage of punches. The Ragman's face was now a bloodied mess as each blow connected with conviction and brute force. In the distance, she could faintly hear the wailing sound of police sirens echoing, cutting through the silence of the night. The sound reverberated through Jessie, sending a wave of comfort, knowing that help was indeed on the way and that this nightmare would soon be over.

In the frenzy of the moment, Trevor never saw in his peripheral vision the Ragman raise his ax. By the time he caught a glimpse of the ax being swung at him, it was already too late. Searing pain surged through every fiber of his being as the ax mercilessly embedded itself in the middle of his back, right between his shoulder blades. Pain, like nothing he had ever felt before, stole his breath away as the world around him blurred. The Ragman stood up, battered and shaken; he callously ripped the ax from Trevor's back, leaving the young man to writhe in pain.

"Leave him alone!" Jessie screamed. "It's me you want; well, here I am."

Unable to help Trevor, Jessie turned and ran, hoping the killer would turn his attention to her. The Ragman walked past Trevor's agonizing body, and with every stride he took, his eyes intensely focused on the young girl. She frantically made her way through the empty aisles, limping along as best as she could. Her eyes scanned the store for anything that could be used as a weapon or a way out. Jessie's heart leaped into her throat as she heard the Ragman's footsteps trailing closely behind. The front doors were still locked, but to her relief, she noticed that Trevor had left the keys dangling in the lock. She lurched toward the door, her trembling hand nervously fumbling with the keys.

The hairs on the back of her slender neck stood at attention as she looked over her shoulder. An ice-cold shiver ran through her spine as her head swiveled just in time to see the descending motion of the ax inches away from her. Her body instinctively moved out of the way as the ax came crashing down through the front door. The sharp sound of glass shattering was deafening; it surged through her ears as broken shards cascaded around her.

Jessie mustered up every bit of strength she possessed and shoved the Ragman away as she scrambled past him. His face was locked with determination as he felt her end was near. He quickly lifted his ax and swung at her again, missing her by a few inches. The sickening thud of the metal blade striking the floor echoed throughout the empty store. Jessie could feel nothing but blind terror; her eyes were wild with fright as she noticed a boiling pot of coffee on a table nearby. Without hesitation, she grabbed the coffee pot, its contents scorching hot, and hurled it at the Ragman.

The pot struck with such intense force that it shattered across his face, sending shards of glass and scalding liquid in every direction. Caught off guard, he let out a horrific scream as his once menacing face contorted in pain and surprise. His grip around the old ax loosened as he stumbled backward and gripped his face in agony. The air in the store, which was once palpable with tension, suddenly became charged with possibility. Jessie's defiant act had given her a momentary advantage, leaving her with a brief chance to seize an opportunity.

The ax made a dull echo as it struck the ground, finally being released from the Ragman's hold. As the lights continued to flicker ominously, Jessie picked up the axe; her hands quivered as she cradled the blood-stained handle. The weight of the weapon settled into her palms as her grip tightened. There was an overwhelming sense of unease and dread that came with holding the instrument of death that had taken her friend's life.

Adrenaline coursed through her body as she raised the heavy ax high above her head. Images of Kelly and Zoe flashed before her eyes as their memories flooded her mind. Innocent and vibrant lives had been tragically snuffed out by a random, senseless act of violence. A part of her wished it had been her instead of one of her friends. In that instant, she decided that their deaths would not be in vain. The overwhelming wave of grief she felt suddenly transformed into furious anger, fueling her movement.

Jessie screamed out a primal roar from the depths of her being. She summoned every ounce of strength she had left as the ax swung down in one swift motion. The blade buried itself deep into the Ragman's skull; the sound of ripping flesh and cracking bone drowned out her own screams. His lifeless body collapsed onto the floor with a heavy thud as she stood triumphant, feeling a momentary sense of bittersweet satisfaction. Deep down, she knew that by taking his life, she would never be able to bring her friends back or undo the damage he had caused.

The sounds of police sirens enveloped the store, filling the air with their blaring, pulsating noise. Exhausted and emotionally drained, Jessie dropped to her knees, her body unable to bear the weight of her anguish any longer. She sobbed with intensity, letting all her pain and sorrow pour out. Trevor, barely able to find his own footing, stumbled through the store and collapsed by her side as officers and paramedics rushed to the horrific scene. In that moment, the world stood still, and Jessie and Trevor found comfort in being alive and being survivors.

The events of that night would be permanently etched and branded in their minds. They would carry the weight of that experience with them forever, cherishing every breath and every opportunity to find solace in the simple act of being alive. They were forever changed by the fateful events of one night... one wrong turn.

THIRTY MINUTES
Kathleen Halecki

The building was grey and square-shaped; reminiscent of brutalist architecture. Enormous cement blocks formed the base, painted in a darker shade of the same dreary color contrasting with a dark burgundy trim along the roof. Soundproof and windowless, it stood on the outside of the city ideally located for those moving in and out. Locked behind an iron gate surrounding the perimeter, it guarded the possession of those who paid for the luxury of having their goods in a secure place. Very few would attempt a break-in as they would be welcomed by a mild electric shock coursing through their body.

People of all sorts came and went throughout the day. None were questioned as to what they loaded and unloaded in vehicles ranging from small cars to large trucks. Boxes of varied sizes, some as small as shoeboxes to those large enough to contain couches and refrigerators were transferred back and forth. Everyone kept to themselves focusing on their goal as they moved swiftly through the garage-like doors that led to the elevators taking them to the upper floors.

Occasionally, the manager would complain to his superintendent that he found someone living inside for want of cheaper accommodations than the city could provide. Sometimes he turned a blind eye if they explained they were only there for a few days until they could gather up their belongings and move into their apartment. Other times he had no choice but to lean in and threaten them with the police for violating the rules of the facility.

Set beside a stone quarry long-abandoned, occasionally wild animals would find their way through the doors only to scurry out when they could not find food or they were shooed away. With few exceptions, the patrons did not worry about their possessions or their security when they rummaged through their storage container. After all, there were cameras and automatic timers locking the gates.

There were codes that were needed in order to access one's floor.

All in all, there was nothing to fear in a storage facility except the horrors of moving.

***

Pushing the last of the boxes from the car into the corner of her living room, Lara furiously turned a lock of long blonde hair around one finger. She pondered the situation, twisting her hair in and out as if it could help her make a decision. Staring at the neatly labeled pile of boxes, it seemed as if her entire life stared back at her. The large black writing on the boxes seemed organized; kitchen, living room, bathroom, and bedroom. Of course, like most people who began their packing in an ordered fashion, there was the dreaded boxes labeled "stuff," consisting of objects thrown in at the last minute in the haste to leave a life that was ending.

She shifted her weight thinking about the last time she saw her belongings. The divorce had been hasty and messy. The large house they once shared was full of the antiques they collected in their travels, some they kept for personal use and others were for their design business. The successful life together ended with her staring at the ceiling alone with just her thoughts to keep her company in bed. The house had been sold quickly, their possessions divided, and she shoved everything into a storage unit before deciding to travel the country deciding what her future looked like alone. Six months came and went and now she faced her life alone.

There were still a few boxes left to move that did not fit into her car on the last trip and tomorrow was the first of the month. As she would not be able to return immediately due to the opening of her new business, she would be paying for yet another month simply for the remains of her life to sit there awaiting her return. She worried that her procrastinating would mean she would be throwing money out the window she could use for other purposes.

Her gaze shifted to the clock on the mantle. It was not yet dark and if she left immediately, she would have time to get to the storage facility and retrieve the final boxes before it got too dark. If she was lucky, she could take everything in a single haul if nobody else was around and the handcarts and elevators remained free. She could make it in and out before the manager ever made his final inspection. She could then call in the morning to finalize the paperwork and move on with life.

Grabbing her handbag and keys, she resolutely set out before she could change her mind. It was better to get it done and over with while she had the energy rather than wait for some unknown date to come.

***

Traffic was heavier than she thought it would be getting out of the city on a late Saturday afternoon. Normally the cars would have been driving in for the nightlife and she spent the extra hour cursing under her breath. She groaned as the last rays of sunshine faded into the sky as she finally reached the long driveway that led to the building. Glancing up, she wondered why storage facilities always looked so inhospitable and ominous. She wished she picked one with windows so she could at least see the outside world.

As she made the turn onto the road, a car moving far too quickly exited nearly hitting her in the process. The near-crash jolted her out of her thoughts as she saw the driver's face through the window in passing. The woman's eyes were wide as if she saw something that terrified her. For a brief moment she hesitated wondering if it really was a good idea to go inside alone wondering what sent the woman away in such a hurry. She tapped her fingers on the steering wheel looking around in the darkness talking to herself aloud.

"It will take you 30 minutes to get in and get out. If you do this now, you will not need to come back again. You are just imagining things. Maybe she hates being in the dark like you do. Stop wasting time and get in there."

Punching in her code for the gate, she continued up to the building and initially thought there were no other cars there but hers. Pulling the keys from the ignition, she locked the door behind her making sure her trunk faced the facility for easy loading. She spotted the manager's vehicle parked on the side and a wave of relief passed over her. She still had forty-five minutes before he made his rounds and if all went according to plan, she would be gone long before he got to the sixth floor. The handcarts were all neatly parked in rows against the wall which meant she would not waste a single moment waiting for one to be returned. Grabbing the closest one firmly by the handle, she pressed the elevator button performing a little jog to pump herself up.

The green light above the frame lit up before she heard the bell and the elevator made a loud thump as it hit the landing. She disliked the metal walls inside as they felt institutional and dirty from the streaks created by various shades of paint and scratches from items that hit the sides over the years. She already put her key into the panel and turned it to allow access to the sixth floor when she detected a pungent odor. It was then she noticed what appeared to be an animal skin in the farthest corner. There appeared to be streaks of blood that went up the side of the wall and she hoped it was not some injured animal that would attack before she could get out.

Cursing herself for going alone and so late, she got as close to the doors as possible in order to make a swift exit. Although the bundle of fur did not move, and made no sound, she could not ignore a fear beginning to swell within her chest.

"Move quickly and all will be well." She whispered to the metal door. "It isn't moving so maybe it is someone's discarded object. Maybe an old woman's fur shawl from decades ago. You are just freaked out by the isolation and whatever that horrible smell is. Thirty minutes, tops, that's all you need and you're out."

The elevator bucked as it stopped and she pressed up so closely that when the doors slid open, the tip of her nose was nearly scraped. The floor was arranged with the elevator centrally located with units branching off in all directions. She surveyed the long rows of metal boxes that seemed to go on endlessly in the dim light from the simple bulb above her. The rest of the lights overhead would turn on once movement was detected. She desperately wished her unit was closer to the elevator rather than towards the back end as she would be forced to pass through the numerous hallways with darkness all around her.

She pulled on the cart and it made a squealing noise that startled her as turned left at the first corner maneuvering around a cement pillar. The lights clicked on echoing a dull buzz throughout the empty floor. She began talking to herself once more for encouragement as she walked down the main aisle.

"Focus on your goal, almost there, just a few boxes and then back to the elevator. Keep going."

The rancid smell from the elevator came in like a wave, stronger and potent, hitting her in the face and overwhelming her senses. Her eyes watered and she froze in her spot, putting one hand to her nose to stop the gag reflex. The odor smelled strongly of wet dog, but it was deeper and more intense mixed with something else like sweat and blood. Head buried in her shirt, she was unsure what to make of it wondering if someone left rotting food in a unit. Her other hand white-knuckled the cart handle as the lights flickered briefly. From behind her, past the elevator on the other side, she heard a deep, rumbling growl. Every hair on her body stood up as cold fear penetrated her bones freezing her to the spot. She blinked trying to peer through the semi-light, her mind unable to come up with an answer as to what was happening.

She heard the sound of banging at the far end of the building first before the manager's face appeared as he stumbled onto the floor in the main hallway pushed from an unseen force. He attempted to crawl away and head towards her trying to grip the floor with bloodied hands. His eyes held hers briefly as he attempted to wave her back.

"Run."

Her flight response did not kick in until she saw what it was he was trying to escape. One long furry hand could be seen hovering midair before the body of the creature appeared. It looked half-man and half-dog as it emerged hunched over in the hall to dig large curved claws into the manager's back.

"Run!" His whisper became a shout and the beast lifted its head, its snout sniffing the air.

Lara broke, in high school she ran track and field once breaking a record in the 55 meter hurdles and her legs soon remembered the strength she possessed in her youth. She realized she would never be able to beat the creature to the elevator as it stood directly in her path. Even if she did a loop around the floor to circle back, she was sure it knew she would head straight for the exit. There were stairs, but those were emergency exits only that unlocked when the fire alarm rang and she was unsure of the nearest box location. She had one chance and that was to make it to her storage unit before it could find her.

Gripping the key between her fingers, she cursed the lights that gave her away as she ran. The manager grew quiet and she knew the creature would soon be on to her. Her shaking hands fumbled as she slid back the face of the lock to insert the small silver key tears forming in her eyes as the lock gave way. As she lifted the latch, she heard the beast snarling as it prowled around catching her scent. She slid through the door wishing it was of heavier steel as the beast came charging around the corner.

When she first took the unit, she noticed two side bolts with hanging chains installed haphazardly on the inside. The manager never noticed when he inspected the unit and she figured someone lived within the space temporarily using the unit in-between apartment rentals. She only happened to notice when one of the bolts caught her favorite blouse when she backed into it moving her boxes inside. She never thought to mention it to management and now it would be the only security standing between her and the creature outside.

She fumbled with the clips connecting the chain to the bolts securing one with her own padlock. She could see the elongated snout sniffing beneath the small gap beneath the door and she held her breath. There was no pretense of hiding and she wondered what it waited for seconds before it slammed its body full weight against the thin steel. The door creaked but held and the beast moved its claws from the top down before hooking them underneath to see if it could lift up. Lara looked for anything inside to stop it as the door moved up half an inch.

The ringing of the elevator bell in the distance caused the beast to hesitate and she crouched down to see what it would do. Some unsuspecting soul, who like her thought only of getting their stored items, was now entering into the lair of a monster. She thought of shouting out to the stranger to stay inside the elevator but before she could do so, the creature took off down the hall and she heard the claws smacking the cement floor running swiftly in the direction of the person who was already out of the elevator.

Holding her hands to her ears, she waited for the screaming to begin for there was nothing anyone could do to protect themselves against such thing. Only a sheet of metal and two bolts stood between her and the whatever-it-was that was tearing apart the man whose voice rang out over the empty space.

***

"I should be home now. Why did I come here against my better judgment?"

Rocking back and forth on the cold floor, arms around her knees, Lara whispered the words over and over again. The thirty minutes she allowed herself had long since come and gone and she was trapped inside with an unrecognizable monster. While she was unsure where it was, she was sure it was lying in wait for her for she could hear the padding of paws as it moved around pacing the aisles.

She was not a woman who gave in to superstition; she always thought she was firmly grounded in reality. She did not watch horror movies, believe in spirits, or read fairy tales, and for the first time in her life she now she wished that she thought such things were possible as it would make the situation seem less unreal. Her brother, Bobby, was a fan of such stories. He went on ghost hunts and engaged in long discussions on supernatural creatures. What would he call what was outside? A werewolf? Were-dog? Beast man? She had no clue because deep down inside, she found it hard to believe that it could exist at all. She contemplated the idea that it was a man in a costume, but it was not possible for a human being to clamp down on a man's shoulder and pull it apart from the rest of the body as it did to the manager.

The image would not leave her mind and she rocked back and forth harder. If she could not figure out how to escape, her death would be the same. The thought of being ripped apart like the others was terrifying. The fangs she saw briefly protruded grossly as it snarled at her, saliva running down the sides of its fur and eyes narrowing to red lights glowing in the hall as it hovered over the manager's body. It was not extraordinarily tall, appearing to be less than six feet, but seemed to possess uncanny strength. So far, although it could take down a grown man, it could not breach the sanctity of the steel and for that she was grateful.

There was no certainty of rescue for her phone was in the pocket of her handbag locked inside her car. Her intention had been to move in and out unencumbered by anything extra and she worried she might drop it as she moved her boxes. Who would believe her anyway if she called to report a werewolf? Realizing she could not sit there, she began to stack the boxes up against the door to add an extra barrier between herself and the beast. Attempting to move things as quietly as possible, she tried to recall the conversations she had with Bobby when he would go on about some of his interests.

Were-creatures; dogs, cats, wolves. Her sharp mind recalled him mentioning the sightings of such creatures in their state although it seemed every state had some sort of local folklore. She laughed when he seriously considered the idea that such monsters existed.

What did he say about them? Think, Lara, think. Something about moons. Moon cycles. Yes, there were moon cycles and there were things you could do to kill it, or ward it off.

She struggled to remember the rest of the information because at the time she half-listened. Vampires could be staked, now that was common knowledge and something she knew from watching Halloween movies with him one year. How did one kill a werewolf? If the beasts lived in the cycle of the moon, she could wait it out until morning when the sun shone and it would return to human form.

Did you see a full moon when you were driving?

She scanned her memory trying to recall the drive there. There was heavy traffic and she remembered the sun going down but she had no recollection of a full moon in the sky that night. She cursed herself for not paying attention.

Too busy being wrapped up in our phones these days to be aware of what is going on around us. What if it is what it is and it retains that shape and continues to kill everyone?

It was something to seriously consider. She wondered why the woman she saw in the car did nothing to warn her. Surely by now she would have reported seeing something unnatural so maybe help was coming soon. Shivering in the damp air she began to despair realizing that she was alone and would be forced to fight for her life. If the beast went on killing, it would take at least a day or two before the missing were reported. It would only be those on the sixth floor who would be devoured. For now, at least, the beast was contained so those on the floors below would be oblivious as to what was happening above them. Unless the creature could understand and maneuver the emergency doors, everyone else would be safe.

A low rumbling interrupted her thoughts while something thick and wet bounced on her cheek. She flinched using her sleeve to wipe it away. Her first thought was water condensation from a pipe in the ceiling but the growl became louder and a wave of foul, hot breath blew across her neck.

Do not look up.

Her jaw began to shake uncontrollably as panic took over. She did not want to meet the ruby eyes or see the drip from the fangs. Using all of her willpower, she swiftly crouched into the corner pushing past the boxes she stacked by the door. Using the largest box as a shield, she lifted her eyes to meet that of the beast. The scream rose in her throat but remained lodge as her breath came in heavy waves. She dug her nails into the cardboard in an attempt to remain conscious.

The beast was balanced along the perimeter that separated her unit and that of her neighbors. Believing she was protected by the door, she never realized how vulnerable she was from above. Somehow the creature understood that the only partition between the ceiling and the storage unit was a metal grate used for ventilation. The unit was not self-contained by sheets of metal and if the beast was able to break through using its teeth and claws to rip up the grate, she would be disemboweled before she had a chance to run.

The beast stopped for a moment to look at her and Lara swore it grinned at her in elation. It was not a wild creature who broke in, but something far darker; a cross between animal and human and it completely understood its motive. It would not be safe on any floor even if she was able to make it to the stairs for she was not sure it could not lift the handle to follow her down.

The beast threw back its head and seemed to howl in delight as it continued to chew at the wire anticipating its next kill. The saliva continued to drip onto the floor as Lara watched, her nails bloody from digging into the rough cardboard.

How do I escape? I will never make it to the elevator. If I try to unbolt the door it will attack me from above. I am defenseless against it.

Her brother's voice popped into her head.

Silver. You kill it with silver bullets.

***

As the beast continued to chew its way through the grate, she watched for any signs of weakness. The fact that it had yet been able to get through the metal was a sign of hope. It was strong but unable to get through the steel door or the heavy wires. It gave her time to think about a plan encouraged by the memory of Bobby's words.

Whether it was a werewolf or not, there had to be something that could kill it. As it was not a full moon, she had to accept that it was some sort of animal, or experiment. If silver killed werewolves and it was not a werewolf, than anything could penetrate the body of the beast. Tipping over boxes as she searched, the creature watched her with narrowed eyes. She quickly surveyed each item for defensive purposes.

She did not have much to work with as she did not possess silver bullets. She did, however, have silver candlesticks brought from France one trip three years ago. She doubted they would be much help unless she could get close enough to knock the creature in the head. As she rummaged through the last box, she finally felt relief instead of anguish. During the last trip to storage she tried to fit the oversized box into her car but it was too long and now she remembered the reason. Inside there were several sets of fireplace accessories. They varied in shapes and sizes, some longer some shorter, but they were all made of iron – but she knew one of them was silver. Purchased from a dealer in Lithuania, the fireplace poker was long and ornate made to decorate the house of a nobleman. She almost laughed at the absurdity of what a gentleman would think now that his poker would be used to kill a werewolf.

Lara focused her energy on survival. She was not going to die trapped in her storage unit digested by a creature that should not exist. The poker felt heavy in her hands and the pointy end was dull with age. Unsure how to proceed, she stood there with one hand wrapped around the poker waiting for something to happen. She placed the key to the lock into her front pocket and placed the silver candlesticks beside the door.

She did not think of herself as brave, only desperate. The beast stopped briefly to watch her before continuing to work through the grate and Lara saw the bits of metal fall to the ground. It would soon have enough room to jump down into the unit and she nearly lost her grip thinking of the claws digging into her flesh. She unlocked the padlock kicking the bottom bolt open with her heel leaving the top one in place until the last moment. If she could steady her courage, and not give in to her terror, there was a small possibility she could make it out alive.

The head of the beast began to emerge through the hole, the snout snapping and drooling in anticipation. The poker was not long enough to reach the creature's eyes and the boxes were too flimsy to stand upon. Lara steadied the poker in her hands; she would get only one chance and if she missed she would be the beast's next meal. Her breath came in great gasping gulps as it began to squeeze its way through the hole inching closer. Using all of her leg strength, she jumped up, poker in both hands, to plunge the silver tip into the beast's left eye, twisting it around as she pulled it out.

Blood spurted throughout the space spraying her face and blinding her briefly as the beast let out a cry causing her to vomit as the sound reverberated around her. As it fell into the unit, Lara reached for the top bolt pushing it back before hitting the oversized head with one candlestick as hard as she could before backing out the door. Reaching into her pocket, she pulled out the lock securing the door seconds before the creature furiously smashed into the side. If she could keep up the speed, she could make the elevator before the beast could either break through the door, or make its way out of the hole in the grate. She desperately hoped that since the elevator last opened on the sixth floor, it was still stuck there waiting.

The beast continued to howl behind her thrashing around the unit in anger and pain. The lights automatically illuminated the slaughter left in its wake. The body of the manager was gutted and blood and skin were splattered on the floor.

Please let the elevator be there. I just need to get to my car.

As she turned the corner past the pillar, she tripped over the last victim whose head, now with unrecognizable features, was propping open the door. Reaching for what was left of the legs, she jumped over the rest of the body kicking the head out of the way. Seconds before the elevator door shut tightly, she caught a glimpse of the beast as it turned the corner, the eye dangling from its socket. The elevator jerked again as it moved and Lara struggled to get her hands into her pocket for her car keys. Her fingers were darkened with blood and she wiped at her face with one sleeve.

Get to the car, get to the car. Once you are in the car you can drive away and call for help.

Rushing out, she noticed another body lying by the handcarts. Without thinking about the situation, she pushed the button to release her doors moving inside quickly as the locks snapped back into place. As she started the engine, she noticed the police cruiser parked near the manager's car, lights still blinking and turning in the night. Turning her neck around, she realized the body lying on the ground was dressed in a policeman's uniform.

Wait. If the beast is locked on the sixth floor how did it get to someone down here?

The woman who passed her must have notified the police who came out to inspect the building while she battled the creature upstairs.

Where is his partner's body?

It took a moment before she noticed movement on the far side of the parking lot when she started the engine. What first appeared to be a person began to approach her at full speed stopping in front of the hood and leaning into the glass. The snout snarled at her as it pressed forward gripping the sides. From behind, she felt the car tip up as a massive shadow appeared in the back window. The creature upstairs was small in comparison to the two who blocked her now, and she could see more of them moving across the parking lot wailing like a pack of wolves. Lara began to sob as the car began to shake back and forth, digging into her purse for her phone.

***

The next morning, Bobby arrived at the storage facility after being contacted by the police. He could see his sister's vehicle, the glass broken and the doors twisted and unhinged. As he waited to talk to the detective who held his sister's bloodied phone in a plastic bag, he noticed an incoming voicemail on his screen. His sister's stricken voice came through on a brief message.

"I'm sorry I ever doubted you. You are right to believe, Bobby, these things are real, all of them."

He covered his mouth with his hand listening to his sister's desperate screams as a chorus of howls drowned out her voice.

Made in the USA
Coppell, TX
15 May 2025